TIES THAT BIND US

Ivy's Passion
&
Cleo's Song

TORETHA WRIGHT

Copyright © 2020 by Toretha Wright
All rights reserved.

Publisher's Note

This book is a work of fiction. Any resemblance to actual persons, living or dead, is purely coincidental. Some legendary people, events, and locations, although accurate, are used fictitiously and derives affectionately from the author's creative imagination.

No part of this book may be reproduced, stored in, or introduced into a retrieval system or transmitted in any form or by any means without prior written permission from the publisher.

ISBN: 9798680658499

Library of Congress In-publication-data

Credits
Blest Be the Ties That Bind by John Fawcett
Excerpt from *Lady, Lady* by Anne Spencer, 1882-1976

Read other books by the author

Ties That Bind Us
Souls On Fire: Four Stories
Reflections in a Faded Mirror (short Short Stories from the deep Deep South
The Secrets of the Harvest
Shadow People (poetry)
Dates and Nuts & other recipes for Romance and Madness Vol. 1
Dates and Nuts & other recipes for Romance and Madness Vol. 2
Black Misery and other Slave Songs

WrightStuf Consulting, LLC, Columbia, SC

www.wrightstuf.com
info@wrightstuf.com

Printed in the United States of America

TIES THAT BIND US

Ivy's Passion
&
Cleo's Song

Part I Ivy's Passion

The First Letter 1

College Life 13

Metamorphosis 29

Giovanni's Room 35

The Last Letter 40

The Meeting 47

Part II Cleo's Song

Prologue 3

Reckoning 75

Small Talk 79

Cold Pizza 82

Six o'clock 91

Willie Walker 100

Reality Speaks Loudly 109

Montel Williams? 119

A Lesson Before Dying 125

Time Out 130

God's Hands 133

Epilogue 136

For Ann

Part I

Ivy's Passion

The First Letter

It was an ordinary morning as ordinary goes. The loud rumbling of the Florence-Audubon freight train forged its way through the small town of Lawrenceville, stirring her from a restful sleep. It was five o'clock. Ivy had longed stopped setting the alarm clock. What for? Some days she'd wished the noisy locomotive would be late or switch tracks and not pass her way at all. However, Old Faithful had yet to veer from its route in twelve years.

Laboriously, she pulled herself from between the warm bed covers and crept into the bathroom. As she gazed in the mirror, she noticed a single strand of silver at the front of her head. Before she could consider what her grandmother had told her years earlier, 'If you pluck a gray hair two grows in its place,' she had yanked it out. "Oh well. It's too late to worry about it now."

She stumbled down the stairway to brew the ritual pot of Maxwell House for her husband while he snored through the jolting and rumbling of the hundred-year-old train tracks. The linoleum on the kitchen floor was cold to Ivy's bare feet. She pushed her feet into an old pair of Reeboks that lay crumpled in a corner by the back door. Her feet enjoyed the warmth as the shoes fit loosely around them. Chill bumps assembled on her arms as she puttered around the kitchen in her sleeveless nightgown. She pulled a gray sweatshirt from the back of a kitchen chair and drew it over her body. The smell of the sweatshirt and the shoes held a warm familiarity. She smiled as she lifted her arms to her face to enjoy the satisfying scent of her husband. The aroma of the freshly perked coffee crept into the bedroom and roused Eric from a deep sleep. He sat straight up in the king-sized bed and groggily called out, "Ivy... Baby!"

Ivy was a long, slender woman of thirty-five, who, by all rights and privileges, appeared to be twenty-five. She had thin long legs and arms, with slim hips and a moderate protrusion of breasts that sagged just a little. The five feet, six-inch frame she was graced with had held up more than adequately over the years, considering she viewed routine exercise as a punishment she'd rather not endure.

Her skin was what some folk called paper sack tan, and it was smooth as satin. The dark, deep-set, sexy bedroom eyes only enhanced her round doll baby face. She had an Audrey Hepburn neck that spoke a swanlike gracefulness. Ivy didn't walk but strolled as if she had somewhere to go but was in no hurry to get there. Smiling was a rarity as there was a seriousness about her that insinuated snobbishness.

Ties That Bind Us: Ivy's Passion

My appointment in Evanston is eight-thirty. Shucks! I'll have to leave an hour earlier. Ivy planned her day while she took a long, hot shower. The steam from the shower always seemed to clear her head and prepare her for the day's journey. *Oh well, hopefully, it won't last too long, and I can get to work.* Besides, she didn't like being thrown from her daily routine. *I'd better wake up Erica and Nikki so they don't oversleep.*

She proceeded to rush. Sweat poured freely from her forehead down her face. "Ahh! Ahh! Calm down, Ivy. Take your time," she said while taking long deep breaths. She washed her face with lukewarm water and placed on a soft cover of loose powder to take away the shine. Deliberately she slowed her pace to avoid the constant flow of sweat that seemed to conspire with her every move. After calm took hold, she pulled on a purple double-breasted, pinstripe pantsuit that she had yanked from the closet. She was dressed to impress. Impress whom?

The certified letter had come two days earlier. She read:

"Mrs. Ivy Brennan . . . Please meet with Mr. George Scott of Stanley, Genwright, and Murray, Attorneys at Law... Wednesday, November 11... 8:30 am . . . concerns a matter of grave importance. . . If you are unable to . . . please call . . . 864- . . . as soon as possible . . . We look forward to seeing you. . . Sincerely . . ."

Thoughts of the letter occupied her mind. "Wonder what this is about?" It seemed odd that someone from a prominent law firm wanted to meet her... and on short notice. It wasn't a summons or some other demanding legal order, yet the wait had been miserable as she tried not to think about it.

The Stanley, Genwright, and Murray law office was in Evanston, almost thirty miles north of Lawrenceville. Eric was a philosophy professor at Evanston College. Ivy wondered if he knew anyone from the firm. She considered asking him to go with her. Then reconciled that thought, it'll be okay.

Ivy had been a legal assistant for Victor Moseley Esq. for the past six years, and his law office was dwarfed compared to Stanley, Genwright, and Murray. Moseley ran a small office that generally handled consumer and civil law cases. Ivy prepared legal papers, mainly bankruptcy filings, and ran the office affairs. She considered becoming a lawyer... most of the time. *I would be an excellent attorney.* However, she had long since ruled out law school or any promise of returning to college. *Maybe if I hadn't married Eric so fast.*

A week after Eric received his master's degree, they were married. Erica was born six weeks later. Ivy was going into her senior year at Bowman. *Single mothers go to law school. I could've applied for grants ... Maybe it would've been tough, but... Ma and Big Ma would've helped. Then Erica couldn't be with me in school... I couldn't leave my baby. Eric probably would have married someone else, anyway. Nikki wouldn't be born... Oh well, things worked out for the best.

With the idea of finishing college on hold – indefinitely - Ivy quietly settled into the position of wife and mother. When Nikki was six, however, Ivy found that she could expand her role to wife and working mother. Job-hunting had been an ordeal for her. She had more doors closed on her than she cared to remember. Rejection letters came in the style of form letters: "Thank you for your interest in our firm, however..." or "Due to your lack of experience in the legal field..." or "As soon as a position that meets your qualifications..." or "We will hold your application on file...."

Suddenly and unexpectedly, one sunny winter morning, she received a call from Mr. Moseley, Esq., offering her the position of legal assistant. That position's annual salary secured almost ten thousand dollars more than the administrative assistant position she was searching for. Ivy sang out a loud, Thank you, Jesus! Without hesitation, she promptly accepted the offer. How odd, she thought, to obtain a job with a firm when she never as much as recognized the name, The Law Office of Victor R. Moseley, let alone applied there. Eric informed her that she had applied to other firms, and they sometimes pass along information of applicants to their colleagues. That analysis left her satisfied.

"I hope Moseley can do without me for a couple of hours today. What in the world could this meeting be about?" She continued to speculate out loud. As the appointment time grew nearer, she became more perplexed. "Why would those top-shelf lawyers want to see me on a matter of grave importance?"

Before heading down the stairway of their stylish A-frame house, Ivy called out to Eric in a semi-loud tone, "Get up!"

He had drifted off into a deep sleep, once more and his uncontainable snoring grew louder and unsynchronized with the songs playing on the radio.

"Get up... it's time to get up, you two," Ivy yelled back up the stairs, this time to her slumbering daughters.

Erica and Nikki were in junior high. Not only had they begun exerting their independence, but they were also insisting on it. Ivy knew their hormones were racing and about to kick into fourth gear. The only things on their minds were socializing and boys... and not necessarily in that order... for both girls... at any given time. The mere mention of a boy they considered fine sent them screeching and screaming into young girl ecstasy.

As Ivy ascended the stairs, she heard the faint rustling of the covers and quietly entered the bedroom. She watched them silently as they stirred underneath. Ivy smiled as she turned on the bright ceiling light and observed her children grumble and pull the covers tightly over their heads.

"Golly Ma, it's not time to get up yet." Nikki protested.

Erica added, "Yeah, what's up with that? We got another thirty minutes to get some sleep."

"No, you don't. Not today. I need to leave early this morning, and your Dad is still sleeping. Get up! Now! Please!"

"Shoot!" Erica was the splitting image of her mother. Ivy thought of herself at fourteen and quivered at the thought of the girls being ready for life's cruel offerings. But who's ever prepared for puberty? She remembered not being ready:

It seemed that Ivy woke up one summer morning and saw round plump breasts had replaced the small hard ones she fell asleep with the night before. She was ten. There was never a period of training. She went from no bra to a size 32B. Going to the fifth grade that year, Ivy had worried that entire summer whether her bra straps would show through her clothes. The following summer, on a hot August morning, she started her period. At the age of eleven, she wasn't ready.

Now her mother's height, Erica was thrilled at the notion of strangers mistaking them for sisters. Although a ninth-grade student, she was taking a couple of senior-level classes. Ivy had prepared her well, but she had doubts about whether she had made a wise decision.

While academically gifted, Erica was socially immature and too trusting. She viewed the world through rose-colored glasses as Ivy once did.

On the other end of the spectrum was Nikki. She had her father's dark brown, suspicious eyes, a mouth with his capricious smile, his wit, and his cynicism, too. She took nothing at face value and would challenge the existence of the sun if she needed to get the point across. Ivy often told Nikki they should have named her Erica instead of her sister since she inherited more of Eric's personality. Often, mother and daughter would go toe-to-toe on one odd issue or another. They frequently debated the subjects of clothes and school, even the weather, if obliged.

Nikki was tall and slender (although not as tall as her sister was) with a dark milk chocolate complexion. Her hair was long, wavy, thick, and jet black, precisely like Gramma Hattie, Eric's mother. Erica's hair had been thick once, but Ivy had introduced her to a perm relaxer early. Her hair never returned to its naturalness, even with the braids both girls donned every summer. Ivy attributed Erica's hair condition to heredity since thinning hair was a trait of most of the women in her family. Ivy, as well as her mother, Iris, and her grandmother, Big Ma Sadie, had baby fine curly hair that became finer with age.

Snatching the covers from both girls simultaneously, she tossed them to the footboards of the twin beds and hurriedly left the room. She heard one of them make their way to the hall bathroom. Ivy yelled, "One of you can use my bathroom, but hurry up so your daddy can shower... and tell him to get up. His coffee is ready... and don't..."

"Okay! Okay!" Nikki said.

Erica added softly, "Okay, Ma,"

Ivy's voice faded as she made her way to the basement. Rustling through the laundry basket, she pulled out a pair of stoned washed blue jeans, a plaid shirt with blues, reds, and greens, a red tank shirt, and her clean white tennis shoes.

The girls showered, put on their terry robes and fuzzy slippers, and headed down the long flight of stairs that lead to the moldy basement, pinching their noses closed as they descended the steps. The basement had a distinct, pungent mildew smell that was stifling at times. This morning the odor was strong and offensive. It had rained the night before and the dampness had settled in.

They had moved the laundry room from the kitchen to the basement to expand the pantry area. Ivy insisted on enlarging the pantry to store the fruit preserves she never had time to make but promised the girls she would do it "next summer." Eric did the reconstruction project with his best friend, Willie Walker. They transformed the unfinished portion of the basement into a service room for the washer and dryer and whatever else they could store there when they ran out of space upstairs. Soon after the renovation, the odor began. The hoses on the washing machine had been loosely connected, and water had saturated the wall and floor behind the laundry room. It had gone undetected for several months and a buildup of mold and mildew from the moisture had set up residence.

When the plumber was summoned to repair the damage, he suggested a germicide solution to rid the basement of the objectionably foul smell. Eric set out several Saturday mornings for Lawrenceville Hardware, but as always, one thing or another sidetracked him. Finally, Ivy said, "Never mind, I'll do it," which she never did. Ivy and Eric adjusted to the odor. The girls didn't.

Nikki's eyes grew wide with disbelief when she saw the clothes her mother had placed in her hand. "No way, Momma, I wore that last Friday."

"It's Wednesday, who'll know what you wore five days ago." Ivy snapped.

With a slow-motion roll of the neck, Nikki countered, "I'll know!" She continued to rummage through the laundry baskets.

Instead of a debate, Ivy gave in with slight hesitation. Time was important! "Well, what are you wearing? Remember it's November... and it's cool... and damp. You need to wear something warm."

Lawrenceville had an exceptionally mild fall, but the temperature had suddenly dropped below fifty degrees, and the last couple of nights, it had dipped to the low forties.

Erica walked to another laundry basket filled with clean clothes. It had been sitting on the basement floor for a few days. She picked up a shirt from the basket and sniffed it lightly. Nodding pleasingly, she pulled out a black knit dress that was more like a long shirt. Ivy conveyed her notorious *'don't mess with me this morning, girl'* look. Erica rolled her eyes around in the sockets and tossed the dress back in the laundry basket. "Ma, are there still some clothes in the dryer?" She asked as she made her way past her mother. She pulled her black jeans and red Mickey Mouse sweatshirt from the dryer and bounced back up the stairs.

"You'll need to run over those jeans with the iron." Ivy's high-pitched voice followed Erica up the stairs. "And Miss Nikki, did you find something to wear?"

Nikki retrieved the Levi's and the tank top from Ivy's hands and asked if she had seen her blue jean jacket. Ivy was surprised that Nikki would wear what she had chosen, modified, of course. She kneeled and pulled an oversized faded blue jean jacket from the dryer. One hard shake removed some of the wrinkles. She leaned over to her mother, gave her a great big bear hug, and sprinted up the steps.

"Hurry up so you won't miss the bus. I have a meeting at eight-thirty in Evanston, and I'm running late.

Eat something, please! And drink some juice! Don't forget to take your vitamins! And make sure your daddy gets up before you leave. He'll fall back to sleep. Bye! I love you ... where did I put my sneakers...?" Ivy said without pausing to take a breath. She ruffled some clothes in the laundry basket, found her tennis shoes, again, and headed up the basement steps.

Remembering her purple eel skin pumps as she headed for the garage, Ivy changed her course. She ran up the stairs to the master bedroom and called to Eric, "Your coffee is cooking. Please get up. I'm on my way out the door." In one quick swoop, she leaned over and kissed Eric on the lips, reached inside the closet, grabbed her pumps, and headed out the back door. It was seven-thirty.

Eric, finally fully awake, said, "Okay, Baby."

College Life

Ivy had been married with children for half her life. She was happily married most of the time but had begun to feel the sameness of life's mocking ties. She had met Eric in the spring semester of her first year at Bowman College. He was a senior and a refreshing distraction. A Political Science major, Ivy went back and forth on whether she would pursue a career in law and public administration. Nevertheless, she had spent the beginning of that freshman year experimenting with those activities she deliberately omitted while in high school.

Briefly, she joined an on-campus political group called Dogma, whose only agenda was instituting coed dorms. Dogma would have preferred a more enlightening cause, but all other 'relevant' causes had been taken on by other campus groups looking to change the world. At least, that's what they said.

The Dogma collection of misfits and potheads concentrated on partying hard and long. Most "members" of this unofficial campus group had been on academic suspension at least once. The majority of its twelve or so participants were capable of the dean's list, and some had made it a few times.

They usually met at an off-campus hole-in-the-wall juke joint, admiringly called the Dungeon, not to be confused with those 'dungeons and dragons' students' hangout.

The Dungeon's business name was Scott's Grill - a one-room dive with a bare cement floor and a broken jukebox that continuously spew down-home blues. Along with the free music came fifty cents hot dogs and dollar draft beer that they whispered tasted like pee. The unisex bathroom permanently smelled of reefer.

Ivy joined Dogma that fall while living in Higgins Hall, the freshman dorm at Bowman College. With only six black girls in the entire forty-room dormitory, Ivy thanked God for the Director of Residential Life. Her request for a 'roommate of a similar ethnic background' came through. Cleo Mitchell was of similar ethnicity. Still, Ivy wondered if their African roots were all they had in common.

Cleo was bold, brash, and hard. Coming to the south straight from Brooklyn, New York, she was loud, cussed, smoked a lot of cigarettes, and drank more bourbon than most men Ivy knew. Cleo was eighteen and looked every bit of twenty-five. She had oily high yellow skin that never boasted even a smidgen of makeup. The dark circles under her big brown eyes set off the crimson bloodshot tint in them. It wasn't that Cleo was unattractive but quite unadorned. Her rather large reddish Afro wore uneven curls and loosely wild, unable to embrace the quality of hair for the ethnic style. She had what Ivy's folks called 'good hair.' Although Ivy would argue with them about what constitutes good hair after meeting Cleo.

She wasn't what you would call fat, but rather unshapely, with enormous breasts that didn't compliment her wide waistline. Her square body gave her stature a shorter appearance than her five-foot-four-inch frame allowed. She always wore a sweatshirt or a T-shirt and jeans that hung too low on her hips. Cleo had arrived at Bowman on a four-year academic scholarship that fall semester, and she brought with her the aggressiveness of the city.

Ivy wondered why Cleo chose Bowman College, an obscure little liberal arts school near the North Carolina Blue Ridge Mountains. There had to be any number of schools higher up on the academic chain that would have gladly accepted a brain like hers. However, Cleo had some social issues, and a small school setting with slight distractions was supposed to help her concentrate. At least that was the advice Mary Burkett, Cleo's counselor from the Brooklyn Home for Girls, gave her when they discussed her future academic plans.

Thus, Cleo introduced Ivy to Dogma, marijuana, and licentiousness. They promptly became best friends. This complex, brazen young woman could curse like a sailor when confronted with life's boxing matches yet cry like a baby when the blows were too hard. But she never got knocked out. Cleo had deep-set wounds. She endured abandonment by her mother and the incarceration of her father. At the age of nine, she witnessed her grandmother's slow death from the impenetrable bonds of cancer. More profound anguish came when Tony, her only brother, was murdered on the streets of New York. He was twenty. She was fifteen. The single ray of sunshine that had beamed through her otherwise dismal world was Mary. Their chance encounter happened while Cleo was housed in one of many foster homes. They forged a compassionate relationship that would endure. Cleo graduated from Holy Cross High School with honors and entered Bowman College without fanfare.

The two roommates enjoyed each other's company. One might say they balanced. Ivy was not above average on the academic scale. Although she was at Bowman on a scholarship, it wasn't because she was studious. Moreover, it wasn't that she was incapable of excelling academically, but she would have had to work for it, and at that point, she'd rather not.

A wealthy Bowman alumnus and writer, Melvyn Dubose, was granting full tuition and board to minority students who showed extraordinary talent in the literary field. Ivy had no actual intentions of considering Bowman, but she accepted the challenge since it included a cot and three hots for free. She had written several essays and won a few contests in high school. Since an English teacher once told her she was gifted with written expression, she thought, Why not? The scholarship mandated a two-thousand-word essay on Essentials of Diversity-America, A Melting Pot, or Tossed Salad. Surprised when the award letter came, Ivy decided to try the accredited four-year institution. If things didn't work out at Bowman, she could always transfer to South Carolina State University. As it was, however, State wasn't offering her a full anything, and a college savings account wasn't a reality. So, off to Bowman she headed with a promise and a 2.5 GPA.

Ivy and Cleo became best friends, despite their differences in appearance and experience. Ivy gained respect for the bold girl whom some called reckless. The hearts of the young women were honest and unpretentious. They didn't have to seek acceptance from anyone. At the same time, Ivy knew that, for all her bravado, Cleo had a sullen vulnerability that most people overlooked.

They struggled through the fall semester of their first year, keeping late hours, drinking, smoking, and indulging in whatever the occasion called for. Ivy did manage to get to most of her classes but found that the classroom was where she received her best sleep. She was amazed at how Cleo could stay out all night partying, drinking, and smoking and remain attentive in class - and take lecture notes. So, it was no surprise that Cleo managed to pass her first semester classes and rescue Ivy from academic suspension.

    College life was a festival for Ivy, and she had returned home to Tyler Town only twice that semester. Iris accepted excuse on top of excuse of why her only daughter couldn't take the two-hundred-and-seventy-mile trip to see her more often. However, Christmas offered no options. She had to go home. Cleo, too, had dismissed all previous invitations to Tyler Town, but Ivy wouldn't take no for an answer this time. Bowman campus closed entirely for the three weeks of winter break, so Cleo reluctantly agreed.

    Ivy knew that Mama and Big Ma would be in the warm, open kitchen cooking and washing dishes and laughing and telling the same stories about the old days. All the women gathered in Big Ma's kitchen for the holidays, even the ones who couldn't or wouldn't cook. Aunt Edna, Big Ma's baby girl, had never cooked or brought a dish to any holiday dinner they ever had as long as she could remember. She and Uncle Mason would come over early with their three stair-step sons, eat breakfast and Christmas dinner, and leave after dark. They would always leave with stacks of plates of leftovers wrapped in warm aluminum foil. Uncle Mason would be smiling and grinning and shaking his head and thanking everybody. He knew that would be the best meal he would eat until another holiday.

Aunt Edna knew she couldn't cook and made no apologies. Big Ma said every woman had her own special gift. Aunt Edna said hers was pleasing Uncle Mason. They would all laugh when she'd strut herself around the kitchen showing off her womanness. She was still petite and pretty after four boys. Her last baby boy was stillborn. She quit after that saying she couldn't take to losing another child.

Aunt Helen, Big Ma's sister, would sit at the large kitchen table in her favorite armchair with the handmade seat cushion and peel white potatoes or sweet potatoes or some other vegetable or fruit. Sometimes Ivy would sit with her for long periods talking about everything while cutting up collard greens or onions or red and yellow bell peppers that had grown in the small garden behind the house. Ivy loved her Grandmother, but she had a special relationship with her great-aunt. Aunt Helen was soft, warm, and always good for a hug or two when Ivy was feeling way down low. She had an air of understanding about her that made you feel safe.

Each holiday brought an abundance of family and friends with it. Ivy's two older brothers, Michael and Anthony Darnell, cousins, aunts, and uncles, would descend on Big Ma's like a flock of wild geese. They all lived a stone's throw away from each other. Big Ma was the center of them all. Her home, lovingly called the Big House, was where everyone congregated during holidays and funerals. Ivy had enjoyed the June summer nights sleeping on the floor of the big screened-in back porch with ten or so of her cousins. It was breezy and incessantly serene. She had lain many wide-awake nights sorting the Big Dipper from the Little Dipper and searching for Orion, a constellation she had read about in school. She enjoyed waking up to chirping blue jays and the early dew fresh mornings with the smell of the honeysuckles that laced Big Ma's sandy backyard.

Ivy and Cleo had arrived in Tyler Town a full week before Christmas. Cleo was already bored. Three weeks without pot, beer, and cigarettes, I'll go out of my damn mind. Cleo thought. However, they relegated themselves to being clean and sober.

Tyler Town was down a hard, unpaved, clay road at the northwest corner of Richland, South Carolina. Together, they had a population of a shadow less than 40,000. Richland was clean for the most part, and the tree lawns were kept neat with seasonal plants and flowers. One small post office and several churches of varied denominations endured in the town. The white Southern Baptists, the black Baptists (there is a difference), A.M.E., C.M.E., Church of God, Church of Christ, Lutheran Synod, Catholic, Jewish Temple, Muslim Mosque, and Kingdom Hall, which you dare not refer to as a church. Iris often said that they had desegregated the South for

Ties That Bind Us: Ivy's Passion

just about everything, except the churches back then. On one end of Main Street, right off Carter Avenue, was the white First Baptist Church. Six blocks away, on Union Avenue, was the black Second Baptist Church, and you knew which was which. Not by the size, design, or upkeep, but by dark brown Jesus in The Ascension on Second Baptist's front stained-glass window.

Most of the 'high riding' blacks of Richland attended Second Baptist Church. Ivy's folks were not considered as such, but they had attended Second Baptist since it was built in 1902. Ivy's great-grandfather, Big Ma's daddy, Deacon Nicholas Tyler, "toted the mortar to lay the first bricks for the foundation of the original structure." That building burned in 1941 and was rebuilt to the grand style it hails today.

Richland had traveled through the civil rights movement with insignificant events. The whites tolerated the blacks as long as they 'stayed in their places.' A distinct line segregated the black from the white side of town. More importantly, there was a distinct separation between the more affluent on both sides of town. What was definitive was that there were few black businesses in Richland before the movement. In that respect, the Colored folks could shop in certain white establishments, but only at certain times. Mixing was done mostly on Saturday when blacks would buy what they needed from stores like Robertson's Department Store or Vilner's Dry Goods. Interesting, however, was the fact that they could buy, but they couldn't try. Whatever they purchased had to be a sure thing because those stores would be hard-pressed to take a return on an item purchased by a Colored.

Grocery buying was different. Like whites, Black folks shopped at the A & P or Colonial store any day of the week. Iris said no one could be that mean not to allow folks to buy food when they needed to. People had to feed their bellies, and you can't put stipulations on when folks were hungry and when folks had the money to buy.

Many blacks had owned their homes, and those who didn't, rented from the ones who did. Like the one doctor and one dentist, the professionals had their practices in the center of the black neighborhood on Union Avenue. Lloyd's Funeral Home was situated in a vast, gloomy, gray-slate tiled, two-story house a few blocks away. The owners, Frank and Essie Lloyd, lived next door in a beautiful brick ranch-style home with an immaculately manicured lawn. Most of the teachers lived in that area, and the small grocery store (with a pharmacy) owned by the doctor's brother was on the corner. Iris and her young, tall, dark, and handsome husband, Joshua Breeland, II, had lived in a modest brick home near Union Avenue with their three children.

The one black high school in Richland was attended by nearly all the county's black high-school-aged students. Two elementary schools were on the east and west outer edges of town. Any association between blacks and whites, except for the school board and other political nuances, had been limited to the domestic workers, who promptly did their labor and returned to their side of town that was, for the most part, simple.

Iris's folks lived in the small farming community of Tyler Town. Her family owned a large portion of the farmland, where they worked small farms, raising pigs and a few cows. The Tylers, first and foremost, farmed fruits and vegetables - corn, collards, sweet watermelons, cantaloupes, beans, and shell peas that they sold from the back of an old 1947 Ford Pickup. Her family rented farmland to a few folks from Richland - blacks and whites. They also rented out a couple of shotgun houses to people who preferred to live in the country but didn't own any land or cared to farm.

Ivy was close to her father, who had worked as an electrician-the first and only black to land a job at the local electric cooperative at that time. Joshua Breeland was a faithful churchgoer and an avid proponent of the civil rights movement. When a local chapter of the NAACP was formed at Second Baptist Church, he joined with fervent anticipation. Together, he and Iris were tirelessly active and spoke openly of the injustices exacted on the Colored. Ivy had understood the chasm between black and white at an early age. What she didn't understand were the contention and racial divisions among the people who looked like her.

When Ivy was about six years old, she asked her father, "Why do the real light-skinned people live in big houses and the dark-skinned people live on the street with the little houses?"

He understood the reality of her question. He answered, "Not all light-skinned people live in the big houses, Ivy. We live in a pretty big house, and you know I'm as dark as they get."

The undertone of Ivy's observance was that not many people of dark color had much affluence. Although Joshua didn't receive any resentment from his lighter-skinned brothers, rather actual or perceived, he witnessed it among others.

Soon after Ivy's social revelation, Joshua was killed while repairing a downed electrical line. Iris took her three young children and moved back to Tyler Town. That was 1965. Thirty years later, there was less of a distinct racial line, but the class line was still heavy and drawn with indelible ink. Like Aunt Helen would say, "The more things changed in Richland, the more they seemed to be the same."

Ivy and Cleo spent the winter break trying to avoid Big Ma, Iris, and everyone else. Paranoia had taken a hard hold of Ivy and hung on tight. She felt on edge and wondered if anyone knew she had smoked cigarettes. Moreover, she was terrified by the notion that someone might smell lingering marijuana in her clothes. Her reaction to questions about college bordered on guilt and mistrust. I wonder if they know, she thought.

Michael, who was generally too eager to be mixed up in Ivy's business, could only spend Christmas Day with the family since he had just started a new job out of town – up north somewhere. Anthony Darnell had married the summer before and felt obliged to spend part of the holiday with his new in-laws who lived a few miles away in Augusta, Georgia.

"Hey, Baby Girl. How is it up in the North Carolina Mountains?" Michael asked.

"Not as bad as I thought it would be."

He continued, "Who is that girl you brought home with you. She looks like she gets messed up. You don't get high, do you?"

"Not really. You know I tried a joint, but it's not me."

"Yeah, right." Anthony Darnell joined in the inquisition.

"What do you mean? Do I look like a pothead?" Ivy asked defensively.

"Not necessarily, a head, but you look like you've been getting into a little something."

"You must be on something, Ant." Ivy returned, halfway smiling.

"Well, all I got to say about it is be careful not to use too much of that stuff. It'll burn what little brain cells you have up. Look at your brother over there."

Ivy laughed. She wanted to confide in them the way she had years earlier, but she couldn't. The solid love she felt for her big brothers had not waned, but Ivy felt a strange distance between them since they all had moved away from Tyler Town. She felt a tense discomfort. Private time with either one of them might reveal her recent escapades.

Both Michael and Anthony Darnell knew their baby sister had been partying, but they didn't realize just how hard.

"Just be careful, Baby Girl," Michael said as he thumped her head and ran the way he did when they were children.

Anthony Darnell grabbed Ivy by the neck and tossed her on the bed. "Be careful. Don't make me come up there to N.C."

Big Ma gave Cleo the third degree while giving Ivy down the country for not calling home more often. She said folks worry about their daughters being away and that she needn't worry her mama needlessly when she had a phone around.

Ivy responded, "Yes, Ma'am," while halfway listening and halfway trying to leave the room. Big Ma was like a bloodhound. She remembered Big Ma finding Uncle Boy's scrap iron whiskey behind the chicken house underneath what seemed like a ton of dried corn feed. She sniffed it out and later beat Uncle Boy like he stole something. He was thirty years old. Ivy thought of what Big Ma would do to her if she smelled anything other than *pure eighteen-year-old girl* on her.

"Who are your people, child?" Big ma asked, "What part of New York you come from?"

The successive firing of questions made Cleo uncomfortable in the room of strangers. She vaguely knew of relatives in Georgia on her daddy's side of the family, whom she'd never seen and doubted if they'd ever seen her. "My daddy is from a town called Calvin, Georgia," she said, hoping they'd never heard of it and would leave it there.

"Oh, my goodness, what a small world," Iris said. "My husband's people are from Calvin. That's down there around Ludowici. A little way up from Jacksonville, Florida."

Out of all the towns that drunk old skunk could have been from, he had to come from somewhere they know. Now they'll never stop asking me these freaking questions, Cleo thought while forging a smile and enduring the affable inquisition.

Questions were thrust upon Cleo from all directions, and they were not meant to obtain clear-cut answers, but to concede caring from Ivy's people. Cleo answered all questions with minimal expression. The only person she found nearly impossible to avoid was Aunt Helen.

"Come and sit down and help me peel these white potatoes, Honey." Aunt Helen motioned Cleo to sit next to her and handed her a small paring knife.

"Alright, but I never peeled potatoes before. We ate boxed mashed potato flakes in Brooklyn."

"Well, child, you're in for some good eating. We country folks try not to eat anything from a box if we can help it." Aunt Helen spoke soft and ordinary. She was a modest woman and never wanted people to feel ill-at-ease around her.

When Cleo wasn't asleep, she was with Aunt Helen, engaging in cheerful conversation and, to the amazement of Ivy, cooking. Aunt Helen was a calming presence for Cleo. Unhealed wounds of painful experiences had been revealed, and Aunt Helen was the panacea. Ivy and Cleo endured those long and daunting three weeks in Tyler Town and returned to Bowman College relieved and with transformed spirits.

Metamorphosis

Bowman greeted Ivy back with a sharp expectation that lifted and enlightened her. The party was over. She refused all invitations to the Dungeon and thanked God and Cleo for her twelve credit hours. She spent more time with her studies and less time with her friend. She was not deliberately avoiding her best friend, but the Melvyn Dubose Scholarship wasn't automatically renewed each year. She needed thirty semester hours by her sophomore year. That meant eighteen had to be earned that spring.

Ingesting knowledge became a way of life for Ivy -at first. She had been wholly attentive to her academic requirements. Until one day, out of nowhere, it seemed, a tall, dark, handsome boy with a guarded smile distracted her. She had noticed him in the library and around campus a few times, but recently he had begun to, if truth be told, stir her passion. She found herself daydreaming about him more than she wanted.

It was a miserable, freezing afternoon. The mountain air was kicking like a bear in tight pajamas. Ivy was on her way to the library when she noticed him walking towards her. Wonder if he's involved with anyone, she thought.

She flirted. "Excuse me. Do you happen to know what time it is?"

He rolled back his coat sleeve far enough to see the face of his watch. "It's almost five o'clock."

"Thanks." Ivy strolled across the courtyard that joined the auditorium and the library. She peered back over her shoulder and noticed that he hadn't moved from that spot where they first made contact, nor had his eyes moved from her as she disappeared from his view. She smiled as his eyes had chased her through the courtyard and into the library. She had been captured.

For the next few days, the same boy would stop and stare as Ivy strolled through the courtyard. Why won't he speak or do something? She couldn't approach him. That would be too forward. Her bag of female wiles was just about empty. Her recent plays at the courting ritual hadn't persuaded him, either. She couldn't think of another reason to approach him that wouldn't show too obvious that she wanted to get to know him. True. Ivy tried to encourage his attention. Yet, she didn't want to operate like some of the girls in her dorm. They went after the guys they wanted with full force. Often, they ended up used or abused - sometimes irreparably. Maybe he's not interested, she thought. Oh, well, so much for romance.

Eric was a fine specimen - the embodiment of good-looking. He had dark brown, smooth skin and the same color all over a hard body. Unlike the sports enthusiasts, she found herself watching on the Wide World of Sports on Sunday afternoon with Cleo, but still nice and firm. A sculpted midriff accented broad, muscular shoulder. High cheekbones and glowing white teeth shared the same face with dark brown eyes that twinkled in the moonlight and glistened through the rays of the sun. From his appearance, he could have been an islander, but he was straight from the Low Country of South Carolina.

"What's your name?"

A voice came out of what seemed to be nowhere and startled Ivy. She turned around and saw the tall, handsome boy standing close behind her. With coolness in her voice, she replied, "Who wants to know?"

"Eric Brennen wants to know!"

"Who's Eric Brennen?"

"Me! And again, you are?" he asked, now more interested.

"Ivy," she responded softly to encourage his pursuit.

"It's good to know the name that belongs to the pretty face finally."

She almost blushed but instead returned, "Really, now? That's not a standard line now, is it?"

"No. Just the truth."

They walked, talked, and laughed all night. Ivy thought about the campus laced with uninteresting boys and how she finally found a nice guy who wasn't a pothead or an oiler like the ones that frequented the Dungeon, although she did recall seeing him there a few times. Eric was a brilliant talker who captured her complete attention. Both were absorbed in each other's presence. They fell in love that night and spent all available time together from that moment on.

Time spent apart was a metamorphosis for both Ivy and Cleo. It was February, and Cleo had experienced extreme weight loss since they left Richland. She looked like death warmed over, Ivy thought. That was an expression Big Ma had used when describing some of the folks in the community who had let themselves go down. It fit her.

Ivy asked, "What is going on with you?" Her approach was less than subtle, but offending Cleo was not intentional.

"Just leave me alone and you and I will do fine," Cleo responded in a way that was not meant to hurt Ivy's feelings and didn't but was meant to get Ivy off her back.

"I'll leave you alone when you stop being such a you know what. You look like hell." The care Ivy started with immediately turned into a scolding.

"Well, I'll be whatever I want to be as long as God gives me breath if I feel like being one. Anyway, don't you have someplace to go or something to do?" Cleo asked sarcastically.

"As a matter of fact, I do have somewhere to go. We have somewhere to go!"

"What do you mean, we?" Cleo asked.

"Let's check out The Isley Brothers. It's only seven dollars, and I got the money from selling our old books. It's enough to get the tickets and a pizza afterward. Want to?"

They smiled at each other the way they used to when they were in harmony. Cleo said, "Let's do it."

The two best friends held each other up. They tried to shield each other, one from loneliness and the other one from naiveté. Committed to spending more time with her friend, Ivy worked hard to lessen her time with Eric. She was relieved when Cleo started to recover the weight that had abandoned her.

Standoffish and even impertinent at times, Cleo became even more withdrawn as Ivy became ever more protective of her. She tried to include Cleo in the time she did spend with Eric, but Cleo declined. Eric and Cleo had limited their conversations to 'hello' and 'goodbye.' They were both blessed with strong personalities. Ivy figured the less communication between the two of them, the better.

Abruptly, Cleo departed Bowman that spring before the end of the semester. It was April and the sweet azaleas were in full bloom. Ivy didn't know why Cleo had left. No one in Higgins Hall knew, either. Ivy repeatedly tried to find Cleo through the Director of Residential Life, but repeatedly her requests were refused. There were speculations that she was expelled for academic reasons, but Ivy knew better.

Through all of Cleo's disparity and mood swings, she was able to maintain at least a 'B' in all of her classes. Rumors circulated among the Dogma crowd about drug charges. Ivy dismissed that rumor, too. Not only had she quit smoking marijuana, but Cleo had given up cigarettes and alcohol (except the Pink Champales). Ivy didn't hear from Cleo again. She spent the rest of her first year avoiding Dogma and academic suspension.

Giovanni's Room

The telephone rang early morning in Cleo's home that rested in the heart of Manhattan on Madison Avenue. "Hello." A sleepy sound breathed into the telephone receiver.

"Hello, Momma. Sorry to wake you up. How're you feeling?"

"Good morning, Tony. I'm trying to feel better. But I want no more needles; I'm tired of those freaking needles." Cleo grumbled as she peered at the clock on the night table. It was six o'clock.

Finally, it was the last of the chemotherapy. Cleo didn't mind the sticking as much as nausea and fatigue that generally followed the treatments. The drug infusions seemed much longer than four days this time. Nevertheless, that part was over, and soon time would tell if the emotional and physical pain she had endured was worth the effort, she thought.

"Well, at least it's over, Momma. You'll be back to yourself in no time." Tony said.

"Yes, you're right. How's the weather down there in Hotlanta?" The question was not meant to be an accurate indication of the climate but more of the culture. Cleo sat up in her king-sized bed that seemed to be swallowed up in the large master suite of her penthouse apartment.

"The weather's okay," he said sarcastically. But it's a little chilly this morning.

"What's the matter, Tony?"

"Nothing. I'm just thinking."

Cleo lay in her bed, silent for a moment, not knowing if she should go further with the inquisition. "What's nothing? Talk to me, son."

"Well, I'm going down to breakfast before we head over to South Carolina, Momma," Tony said in an apologetic tone. "I'll call you when we get to the office."

"I wish I could be there with you." Cleo had waited for this day for seventeen years. She thought it mocking that circumstances would not allow her presence.

"I know. I'll be all right. Get some rest, Momma and don't worry."

"Call me."

"I'll call you when we get there. It's only a couple of hours."

"Who's picking you up?"

"Mr. Scott sent two nerdy-looking dudes from the firm over here. They're waiting on me down in the dining hall now. I'll call you. I have to go."

"Tony, I love you, son."

"I know, Momma. I know... I love you, too."

This was Tony's first year at Morehouse College. He had graduated from high school a full year earlier than the norm. However, he wasn't the norm. He had done everything before the norm. He rolled over, sat up, walked, and talked before the norm. Overjoyed by his successes - academic and otherwise, Cleo was less than thrilled about his leaving home at just turned seventeen. This was her baby boy and she wasn't ready to let him go - to release him in a society that considered him unessential for the most part. Cleo thought about her time at Bowman College. That was a long time ago. Compared to her present life of wealth and familiarity, she believed her time at Bowman was an adolescent awakening. She slowly reclined against her soft goose-down pillows. She reminisced of how she had infrequently ventured out of the state of New York until that seven hundred and twenty-seven-mile trip to the mountains around Asheville, North Carolina. She remembered every turn, every road, and every *Welcome to the State of*____ sign as if she had traveled the day before.

Mary had rented a red Pontiac Le Mans. The inside was packed with stuff like potato chips, Oreo cookies, and Shasta Orange sodas. Jet and Ebony magazines and paperbacks, with titles like *Another Country* and *Giovanni's Room* by James Baldwin, had come along for their pleasure. Pillows, linen, and clothes were packed tightly in the trunk. An array of miscellaneous items they couldn't name if you ask them, but swore they were crucial, were crammed on the back seat. From Queens Village on Hollis Ave, turn right onto 217th Street, bear left onto Hempstead Ave, then right on some local road to Jamaica Ave, then left, continue to 212th Street to Interstate 295 to the Jersey Turnpike, through Pennsylvania, Maryland, West Virginia, Virginia, Tennessee and finally to North Carolina. Cleo was apprehensive about going to school down south. She didn't know a soul in North Carolina nor the surrounding states. She had heard of paternal roots in Georgia but had never set foot on southern soil before entering Bowman College. Mary had convinced her to try it out since a full academic scholarship to an accredited college was not just handed out on the street.

The first day Cleo entered Higgins Hall was the first day she met Ivy. Her first impression of the southern girls was idiocy. They were overly pretentious, and it was difficult for her to disassociate the few blacks from the whites. To Cleo, their twang speech was unnerving, and their apparel was boring. *What have I gotten myself into?*

Nevertheless, an instant bond developed between Ivy and Cleo. Ivy was different in an interesting way. She was pretty but didn't seem to notice it much. They celebrated college life with shared enthusiasm. For Ivy, Bowman College was an experiment in living away from the confines and constraints of a small town and a close-knit extended family. Cleo viewed it as a barrage of rules and restraints that she broke with enthusiasm each chance she could.

That was life then. Life before she realized that living had strange twists and turns that always bring you back to the place you start out. No matter how hard you try to get away -far away- like a boomerang, you come back to that beginning. And you always come back harder than you left.

The Last Letter

Twenty minutes past eight! Ivy entered the spacious and stylishly decorated office of Stanley, Genwright, and Murray. Puzzled! Why in heaven's name am I here? This pressed on her mind.

The young, perky receptionist knew Ivy as soon as she approached her. "Good morning, Mrs. Brennan," she chirped, rising from the large antique cherry wood desk. "Please walk this way."

Ivy launched a mischievous grin as she struggled to refrain from laughing aloud. She imagined herself mocking the vivacious receptionist's bouncy walk. Now somewhat relaxed, she followed the receptionist to a large boardroom. The walls in the room were lined with large wooden framed pictures of old men who looked stalwart and stuffy. The room was old and cold, with furnishings of very heavy dark woods. This was a far cry from the law office of Moseley, Esq., which was housed in an old, but stately renovated house on Lawrenceville's Main Street.

"Coffee, juice, or can I get you something else, Mrs. Brennan."

"No, thank you... I'm... I'm okay." Her uneasiness resurfaced.

"Well, please have a seat, and Mr. Scott will be in shortly."

Ivy was restless. "Eight thirty-five!" She mumbled as the grandfather clock ticked louder and louder. Thoughts of Moseley moved through her mind. She remembered what she had told him. I'll be in around ten.

It would be possible to get to Lawrenceville in thirty minutes if she took the interstate... and left now. Lawrenceville was only twenty-three miles west of Evanston. She had clocked it on the way there. But what if this is a job offer for more money than what Moseley is paying, she thought. Why would a prestigious firm like this want to hire me and for more money to boot? She scoffed at such a ridiculous notion. Moseley paid Ivy a hefty forty-five thousand dollars a year, and bonuses when large cases came their way. She had gotten five bonuses in the six years she had been with the firm. One bonus was more than five thousand dollars. Eric had gotten jealous and asked her if she was having an affair with the old man. Moseley was old and looked it. Nevertheless, he could run circles around the younger lawyers he came up against in anybody's courtroom. She thought of how generous Moseley had been to her over the years and felt like she was betraying a friend.

The boardroom was large and cold. The longer Ivy she sat alone, the larger and colder the room became. Feeling small and insignificant, she wondered if she should walk out. Silently, she rehearsed her exit speech. Miss, I can't stay any longer. Please let Mr. Scott know that I had another appointment and couldn't wait.

"Mrs. Brennan." A deep voice entered the room. "My name is George C. Scott, not the actor." He laughed sheepishly at the suggestion that Ivy might even know who George C. Scott, the actor, was.

Ivy knew George C. Scott, the actor. Personally, it seemed. Patton was a regular on the bedroom television in the early morning hours when Eric couldn't sleep. However, Ivy was less interested in George C. Scott, the actor, rather than the attorney, at that point. She waited for his next line and hoped it was less comedic and more informative. Ivy glanced down to view her watch in a manner that instructed him to get on with why he had summoned her. Mr. Scott stared at the woman as if he couldn't believe she was the same Mrs. Brennan he had ask to come to his office. Ivy looked younger than her years and carried with her a childlike innocence. She stared back at the tall, black-skinned sophisticated man. Still silent, Ivy stood up proudly, insinuating she had enough, and swiftly proceeded to leave the office. As she approached the door, a handsome young man of about seventeen years entered the room.

"Excuse me!" They said simultaneously, almost crashing into each other. They were face to face, and an air of familiarity abounded. Who was this tall, dark brown boy with the suspicious eyes?

Five men suddenly converged in the room. Two were dressed in neat, dark blue suits, the kind the IBM people wore in the eighties with the starched white shirts. They all gathered around the large conference table. Mr. Scott slowly walked close to where Ivy stood, overwhelmed. He gently took her arm, leading her to the seat at one end of the conference table. She stared at the handsome young man and then glanced at the others.

"What is going on?" she said in a loud voice. "What is this about?" she continued even louder.

Mr. Scott said, "Mrs. Brennan. Let me apologize for the secrecy and the way this matter has been handled. A week ago, we received a call from New York, Manhattan, to be precise. We were asked to assist in a legal matter that would have a significant financial impact in our jurisdiction."

He walked around the conference table and pointed to the young man that seemed out of place with the others. "See this young man? His name is Tony..."

Ivy interrupted. "And what does that supposed to mean to me?"

"Mrs. Brennan, please let me finish."

"Get to the point!" Ivy's attitude bordered on rude - an attempt to mask insecurity.

"Right!" Mr. Scott said, trying to assert a professional presence. He pulled a sealed envelope from one of the files stacked on the end of the conference table and placed it in front of her. Without an exchange of expressions, Mr. Scott, Tony, and the men in the suits left the room.

Ivy carefully examined the sealed envelope. She took the brass letter opener from the corner of the conference table and opened it. The heading read:

The Stanley Foundation, The William Penn Building, 1134 Madison Avenue, Suite 37E, New York, New York, 01011.

Dear Ivy, I know this letter is a shock, to say the least. First, let me say I have missed you these past seventeen years. I always hoped that I'd pick up a newspaper or a magazine and read that you did something great. However, knowing you, I know you're thinking, "I did do something great." And you did! You married Eric and had two beautiful daughters. Yes! I kept up with you over the years. I knew the day you got married. The white dress was a bit hypocritical, if you know what I mean, especially with the big gut and all (smile). I even knew the trauma that Erica went through at birth and how you'd said she was the last one. Then along came Nikki. Yes! I missed you so much and wanted to share those happy times with you, the sad ones, too.

I knew when Big Ma had the stroke, and you were torn between moving back to Tyler Town to help Iris or staying with Eric. He was going through the seven-year itch, but he loved you and always did. Sure, he looked, but I'm doubtful he touched anything but his imagination. You know how egotistical he is. Ivy, I'm sorry I never called you in all these years, but I couldn't. I hope you can understand that it was better that I didn't. I was sorry to hear about Aunt Helen. She was a nice woman. I only met her that Christmas, but she was so kind to me. Remember! She gave me a Christmas present, and she didn't know me from Adam. You know how much I loathed Avon, but I wore that 'To a Wild Rose' scent to death...

Ivy adjusted her seat without taking her eyes off the pages. All her concentration rested on the letter.

... By the way, how is Moseley? Yes, Moseley. I'm bringing up all of this because it will help explain why I never contacted you. I knew you only for a short while. But within that time, you were my sister. You could've made friends with anyone at Bowman. Yet, you were my best friend. That was a hard time for me. I'd never been down South before and I didn't know what to expect. You were there with your heart wide open and innocent and I liked that. But I got to tell you that sometimes your gullibility amazed me. The city would have swallowed you whole.

Ivy was out of her seat and pacing the floor in anticipation of what was next. She found herself anxious to get to the end quickly, but she clung to every word. She couldn't omit a single syllable.

...let me get to the point but bear with me. This is a difficult time. I'm fighting to find the right words. By now, you must have met my son. His name is Tony. I named him after my brother. He's a good kid and I'm proud of him. Ivy, here's the hard part. I've struggled with this for seventeen years and I know I must face it now. The only way to explain it is this way. First, I'm sorry for the heartache this will cause. Second, it was no one's fault. It was just one of those things...

Ivy placed the letter on the table and walked to the window. She looked out to the street as the traffic seemed to roll by in slow motion. Ivy was relatively happy with her life. She had a husband whom she loved and who loved her. They were more than comfortable together. Her girls were bright and good-natured. Although they were going through the upheavals of adolescence, she could contend with their fickle behavior. The mortgage was more than they could realistically afford, but they managed it. Her eight-year-old white convertible SAAB 900 was on its last lap and her wardrobe needed a thorough overhaul. Nevertheless, she felt blessed and didn't want anything to dishevel the nest.

Without as much as a small indication of her intentions, Ivy snatched up her briefcase and left the boardroom. As she exited to the lobby, she glanced over her shoulder. Mr. Scott followed her to the elevator with a look of confusion on his face. Ivy then left the office of Stanley, Genwright, and Murray.

The Meeting

The small liberal arts college in Evanston had been a refuge for Eric. He enjoyed his academic surroundings and avoided the political milieu as much as possible. He was not pressured to write academic papers but did so at his own pace. Eric was about teaching from a humanistic point and captivated his listeners with theories of his own persuasions. Though somewhat of a ham, he had the gift of teaching. Charismatic in his delivery, he was more than well-liked by his students and respected by his peers.

For ten years, he had managed to avoid the trepidation of publishing a full-blown academic textbook. He had many papers in publication and one had given him some notoriety. National Public Television had aired a program based on his paper, *The Antimonial Society*. This paper challenged the reality of moral law against blind faith in American society. Eric's own belief was that man had sole responsibility to his own fate by obeying moral and civil laws.

He felt that no matter what circumstances we were born into or find ourselves in at any given point in our lives, we were responsible for our maximum potential in living up to God's laws. He said that God was not seeking perfection because we are not created as perfect creatures. All that is required of us is our best, which is not the same for every man. However, God's empirical laws are the same for all, and by that measure, we are judged.

Ivy had sat in on Eric's lectures on many occasions. She enjoyed the discussions on the resurgence of metaphysics among many New Age scholars. They often had intellectual exchanges on the ultimate significance of the universe. His view was reality could only exist in matter. Her belief was reality first exists in thought by way of the heart, and consequently, in matter. And without this order of events, reality would be intangible. They were like oil and water. They shared their lives together, yet neither lost their distinctions.

It was nine forty-five when Ivy arrived at the Evanston College campus. Eric would be in class until ten-thirty. Forty-five minutes was too long; she had to tell him about the meeting at Stanley, Genwright, and Murray. At the same time, Ivy knew it would take another hour to get back to Lawrenceville. Moseley knew she would be late, but not this late. She sat in the car for a few minutes, debating whether she should drive back to Lawrenceville and talk to Eric that night or interrupt his lecture. Wednesday night was Eric's late class night. He wouldn't get home until ten o'clock or later.

Ivy marched down the long walkway of Gillian Hall with purposeful strides. Her thoughts were on the meeting with Mr. Scott, the men in the suits. And the boy. She didn't notice the blue-green lawn grass as usual. She had always commented on how the campus yard was nicely manicured and how Evanston's college catalog cover was one of a few that didn't exaggerate its serenity and beauty. Even the old baroque-style buildings didn't show deteriorating signs of their one hundred and twenty years.

Ivy sought Eric's attention through the half-glass door of the classroom. As he walked through the door, he smiled as he heard whispers of compliments from some of the students. He protruded his chest farther as one male student called Ivy a pretty young thing.

"Hey, Baby! What's up?" Eric casually said as he exited the classroom, closing the door behind him.

Ivy walked closer to Eric as if feeling his breath on her skin was more comforting. "I need to talk to you!"

"What's wrong, Ivy?" Eric grabbed her upper arms, gently shaking her. "Are the girls all right?"

"Oh, yeah, it's not the girls. Eric, I saw someone today and it was so unreal. I can't believe it."

"Who? Who did you see? I thought you were going to see some attorney downtown."

"I did."

"Well, what happened?"

"Do you remember my roommate at Bowman?"

"Who, Sharon?"

"No! No! Cleo. Remember, she left Bowman before we got out that spring, and I didn't know what happened to her."

"Yeah, that wild Cleo. You saw her at the lawyer's office?" Eric said, relaxing somewhat and leaning on the wall.

"No! Mr. Scott gave me a letter she wrote to me ... and I saw her son. His name is Tony. She named him after her brother. You know I told you about him. He was killed when he was about twenty. Anyway, Eric, it was as if I saw a ghost from my past. I have never felt so ... so. I don't know. Freaky. I was glad to hear from her, even in a letter... and to see him, but I was upset. She never called me or tried to get in touch with me in all these years. She just up and left Bowman... I know I didn't know her long, but I knew her. She was my best friend... like a sister. And she springs back on me now."

"So, what was in the letter? What happened? Where is Cleo?" Eric probed for an-swears that he knew were not readily available.

"I don't know where Cleo is... I didn't finish the letter. I left before that Mr. Scott could tell me."

"Do you want to know where she is?" he asked sympathetically.

"Yes! I guess. She's been keeping up with us all these years! All that stuff in the letter was about us. It was kind of weird. Why couldn't she call or write or something to let us know she was okay."

"Well, that's probably in the letter you didn't finish reading," Eric said a bit cynically.

Ivy felt foolish. Why did I leave like that? She thought how abruptly she had fled from the office. "Ride back there with me, Eric."

"Okay, Baby, let me take care of my class. Give me five minutes."

"I hope they're still there."

Eric dismissed his class early and left Evanston College with his wife.

The drive to Stanley, Genwright, and Murray seemed long. It was a fifteen-minute ride at best. Ivy was awkwardly silent as they both gazed straight ahead. Eric reassured her that once they found out what the meeting was about, she would feel better. He wasn't reassured. He was curious now more than ever.

Eric wondered, what's Cleo up to?

As they parked in the multilevel parking garage, Ivy leaned over and gave Eric a tender kiss on the mouth. He reciprocated with a warm hug. They sat wrapped tightly together. Ivy thought how especially close she felt to Eric at that moment. He had not been her protector for years. She had developed the attitude that she could take care of herself. Ivy had said that if Eric got a wild hair up his butt, she would leave him and do just as well without him. Many self-sufficient women she knew engaged in the usual conversation. They say things like the man was needed only for home maintenance and car repair. However, deep down in the well of her soul, she knew she needed Eric for his emotional strength and a level head. At that very moment, Ivy had been exposed. Her need for him had gone beyond all bonds of affection.

Eric approached the receptionist area with Ivy pinned close to his side. She noticed that an older gray-haired woman, less personable, had replaced the cute, bouncy receptionist.

"May I help you?" The woman stated it more than asked.

Ivy was silent. Waiting for Eric to take charge, she searched the room for a familiar face. There was none. The office had been vacated, except for an unkempt young man, watering the sizeable green foliage, which both seemed roughly out of place in the staunch surroundings.

Eric replied, "Mr. and Mrs. Eric Brennan to see Mr. Scott."

"Is he expecting you?"

"Please tell him that Ivy Brennan is here to finish her appointment." Ivy's confidence was returning.

Ties That Bind Us: Ivy's Passion

The receptionist, though confused, leisurely walked down the hallway, smugly peering over her shoulder at the two of them. She disappeared in an office that seemed miles away. Eric anxiously paced the floor like he had when Ivy was in difficult labor with Erica for nineteen hours. However, a great peace had come over Ivy. She was calm as she stared down the empty, dimly lit hallway.

After a brief absence, the gray-haired woman reappeared in the hallway, motioning the couple to join her.

"Come on, hurry," she said with agitated firmness.

Mr. Scott was alone in the immaculate room. It was overly neat and almost too clean. Even the drapes at the window hung with precision. There were no papers or files in sight. One wall housed extended shelves that held law books in an organized manner that seemed almost false as if they had been painted on. Not even a pencil holder crowded his desk. A small paperweight of a shark lay on one corner of the cherry wood desk. On the other side was a photograph of a young woman draped in cap and gown, holding her sheepskin. One could assume this young woman to be Mr. Scott's daughter. If only for the mere fact that she looked exactly like him, except with a quiet femininity

He reared back comfortably in his oversized black tufted leather swivel chair. His hands were loosely clasped together. He imposed a contemplative gaze upon the couple and wondered if they could survive the challenge that was about to occur. The comedic mannerism he had displayed earlier that morning was replaced with a straightforwardness.

"Please sit, Mr. and Mrs. Brennan."

They sat in the two chairs that were aligned precisely in front of Mr. Scott's desk. They seemed to have been placed there, especially for them. The room seemed silent without end. One party impatiently waited for the other to speak.

Finally! Ivy broke the chilly quiet. She cleared her throat as if stalling until the words she needed freely emerged. "Mr. Scott, please excuse me for running out on you this morning. This, all of this caught me by surprise."

"I understand." Mr. Scott said in a genuinely sympathetic voice.

"We can finish the meeting, but my associates have gone to lunch. Can we meet at one?"

Eric intervened. He peered at the man behind the big desk. "Do you still have the letter?"

"Yes, but..."

"Well, can we see it?"

"That'll be a little awkward."

"Why? The letter was written to my wife."

"Yes sir, but there has been a change in plans..."

Ivy asked. "What change?"

Ties That Bind Us: Ivy's Passion

Mr. George C. Scott walked from behind his desk and to the door. "Mrs. Brennan, I'll see you and your husband in the conference room at one o'clock." He quietly closed the door behind him as he departed down the opposite end of the hallway.

They waited quietly. Neither took their eyes from the floor, and they searched for answers in the comfort of each other. It was eleven o'clock. The hands on Ivy's watch seemed to move scarcely. She thought of the contents of the letter and wondered where Cleo was. The memories of her friend made her more anxious. She wished she had been more courageous.

She remembered the last time she saw Cleo. The southern spring air was warm with relief from the Blue Ridge breeze flowing in and out. A strange sense of calm overtook her, and she smiled.

Eric cleared his throat only to break the silence. They sat there still and without words. He glanced around the room for a magazine or a book or something to ease the time. He saw the law books styled neatly on the shelves and scoffed at the rigidity of the place. Two hours is a long time to idle away, he thought. "Ivy, let's get some lunch. We can be back before one o'clock."

Hesitantly she agreed.

Mac's on Main was a quaint little sandwich shop directly across the street from Stanley, Genwright, and

Murray. The lunch crowd had just started to come in. Eric was glad they had gotten in just under the wire. He ordered the lunch special of Ham and Swiss on Rye Bread with Potato Salad and sweetened ice tea for both. Ivy remembered she hadn't eaten all day. Generally, she picked up cinnamon and raisin bagels and coffee on her way to work to share with Moseley. Ivy wondered if Moseley had eaten. There was uneasiness in her stomach, but she couldn't distinguish the pangs between hunger and nerves. They sat at the booth by the window. Not saying much, they ate, only commenting on things they observed on the street. Ivy noticed that the sky had an odd azure blue color. She couldn't recall ever seeing that color before. Then she remembered that same sad color blue sky that day her daddy died. They finished their meal and returned to the Law Office of Stanley, Genwright, and Murray.

Finally, the clock that sat on Mr. Scott's credenza chimed at one o'clock. The sudden tap on the office door startled the couple. The perky receptionist entered and said, "Please walk this way," as she led them out.

Ivy laughed and whispered to Eric, "Let's walk this way." She swayed her hips sharply from left to right.

Eric didn't share his wife's amusement. He grabbed her waist to curtail her mockery and followed her into the cold conference room.

Mr. Scott greeted them with his usual charm. He smiled and asked if they would be seated in the two chairs positioned next to the head of the conference table. Although the morning meeting hadn't gone as planned, they'd recover. "Every good barrister worth his salt should always have a contingency plan that's workable."

"Mr. and Mrs. Eric Brennan. Attorneys Ronald Delaney and John Washington."

Ivy glanced across the table at the two men in the neat blue suits she had seen earlier. They were more affable now. Relaxed! Mr. Scott's introductions of the other men seemed to eliminate the awkwardness in the room.

Nevertheless, each party nodded in a manner that notified the other that their meeting was perchance, and they would probably never meet again. Any display, other than mutual politeness, would be a waste of everyone's time.

Mr. Scott motioned to the young man who stood quietly in the doorway, waiting to join them. "Mr. Brennan, this is Tony Mitchell."

Eric had failed to acknowledge the young man's presence earlier. Tony moved towards him. "Pleased to meet you!" Eric said as he extended his hand to greet him.

"Likewise." Tony's grip was firm.

The table that had held the silver coffee urn had been replaced with a rolling butler of soft drinks and a large sterling silver ice bucket and fine crystal. "Could I get you a cola or ginger ale?" Mr. Scott asked.

"A Coke with a couple of ice cubes. Thanks." Eric's mouth was dry like yarn.

"The same for me with more ice. Thank you," said Ivy.

"Well, shall we complete the business at hand?" Mr. Scott opened a portfolio and placed a manila folder on the table.

Finally, I'll finish the letter, Ivy thought. She waited for Mr. Scott to pull it from the folder. Instead, he walked to the conference room entrance and greeted a woman with large brown eyes.

"Cleo!" Ivy stood but could not force herself to move further. Her chair tilted sideways and fell over. Then silence. She waited for someone, anyone, to speak. No one spoke – with words. Eyes spoke. Ivy's eyes expressed joy and fury. Cleo's eyes informed dismay. Yet, the room held an overt stillness – not calm, but a quiet that comes before a wild tornado.

Eric interrupted the still as he placed the chair upright. Mr. Scott escorted Cleo to the conference table as the men stood up to greet her. Ivy examined her friend, the darkness of deep-set eyes that spoke a familiar sadness. She felt a chill that filled her bones and traveled the length of her body. Sympathy replaced silence, and empathy replaced anger. Underneath the perfect cast of makeup and the well-coifed wig was a very sick woman. Ivy remembered that same weary look on Aunt Helen as she hugged her old friend. Cleo tried to suppress a grating cough, but she conceded as Ivy released the frail body that was once so fleshy.

When Ivy took a firm hold on Cleo's bony hand, the silence was lifted. "How have you been, Cleo?"

The answer was terribly apparent. That instance, Ivy ventured to utter all the difficulties she had repressed for years. Those repressions that only God and your best friend were entitled to hear. There was so much to say. Good things to share. She wanted to tell Cleo everything about her life... her job... her children. She wanted to tell the whole lot - since the time she last laid eyes on her. Most of all, she wanted to say to her that she loved her and missed her. At once, all uncertainty dissolved and was replaced with that same maternal aspiration she held seventeen years earlier.

Cleo released a faint reply, "I flew down when George told me you had a hard time with the letter. I'm sorry." Her voice faded in and out.

"Don't be sorry. I wimped out. I should've finished it before I rushed out. That was stupid." She continued after a deep breath. "You said you took a flight. Where from, Cleo? Where in God's name have you been?"

Cleo realized that Ivy had picked up exactly where they left off seventeen years earlier. The tone in

Ivy's voice rang reminiscent. Cleo remembered all those times Ivy had hauled her over the coals for staying out all night. She was delighted and forced a mischievous grin.

"I flew in from New York this morning. As a matter of fact, we just arrived, straight from the airport." She was reluctant to say in her private jet.

"I'm sorry you had to do that, Cleo."

"You know, I'm glad I did. We can get everything out in the open, face to face."

"What do you mean? Everything out in the open?" Ivy asked. "Tell me. Tell us what's going on with you..."

The lingering anticipation caused Ivy's frustration to rejuvenate. Eric grasped Ivy's hand, gently holding it. He remained silent through the courteous yet annoying exchange.

Mr. Scott quietly left the room. Tony and the two attorneys followed. Cleo and Ivy stared at each other briefly before breaking out in a clamor of laughter. They were genuinely happy to see one another. Whatever fate had brought them back together after all these years had to be a spiritual reward, Ivy thought.

Eric said, "Y'all haven't changed a bit." He said it, but he didn't know if he meant it. As he stood amid them, he saw they had changed.

Through her reminiscence, Ivy recalled events she hadn't thought of in years, and before today would have preferred to keep them housed somewhere in the dark recesses of her mind. Things like the Boone's Farm Party, where they won a 1966 Chrysler New Yorker on a bet that they could out-drink two guys from Reid Hall. They killed a case – just the two of them. Although they never received the title, they drove the car until Ivy backed it into a utility pole, blacking out a third of the campus. They told similar stories, some that embarrassed Eric. Others that made him remember, too. "So, what's happening with you these days, Cleo?" He asked to quiet the uneasy hilarity between the two friends.

Cleo's smile faded in the coolness of his question. The quick change in her behavior caught Ivy off guard.

"What's the matter, Cleo?" Ivy was confused.

"I might as well say it."

"Say what?"

"Say what you came to hear. Say what I flew down here to say."

"Well, go on and say it, Cleo." Ivy was anxious to know that part of the letter she left unread on the boardroom table.

Cleo announced, "Eric, Tony is your son."

The resounding joy that was upon the room only minutes before, had vanished. Disbelief had replaced it -- uncomfortably. Eric gazed at Ivy like a wolf caught with a fresh hen in his mouth. He didn't speak. He waited for her to either speak or permit him. Ivy's blank stare indicated that she didn't know what to say, yet. She remained silent.

The back of the chair supported the full weight of Cleo's weak body. As she looked in the direction of the couple, her eyes were only on Ivy. Waiting for eye contact, Cleo needed an open heart, as well as an open mind for what she had revealed.

"Eric is Tony's father!" Cleo exclaimed firmly. She waited for the reaction that failed on her first admission. Silence hung heavy throughout the room like storm clouds. "We had a brief affair that turned into a life."

Raising her eyes to the point of direct contact, Ivy asked Cleo cynically yet with genuine curiosity. "When and where did this brief affair occur?"

Cleo answered with humility and grace, "Ivy, it was before you met him. You had gone home for Thanksgiving."

Eric stood up. He placed his hands in his pockets and walked over to the window. Quiet.

"I had seen Eric at the Dungeon a few times. One day a bunch of us was involved in one of those idiots' discussions. You know the ones where someone says something totally off the wall and a debate followed." Cleo continued the unrehearsed speech as her weakened body insisted that she stop. "Well, this time, Eric came in and joined the bull."

Ivy managed her attention through the pervading fury that crept up on her.

Cleo went on, "He started speaking. I don't know why, but everybody shut up and listened to him for a long time. Afterward, we talked... about different subjects - art, movies, and all kinds of things. It was refreshing to talk to someone who had actually read a translation of *The Iliad* and not just Cliffs Notes."

The weight of the confession took a toll on Cleo. She pulled out the chair that had been her pillar and sat down. Ivy moved farther away from her friend. She was mixed with the aggravation of this bomb that had dropped on her so cavalierly and the anticipation of where this revelation was headed – yet oddly, she wallowed in the anticipation.

"Anyway, the following night, Eric was there. He was talking about Richard Wright's Native Son. You know that was my favorite novel, Ivy. Well, we, Eric, and I, went off to ourselves and started talking about a lot of stuff. It was one of those things. You meet someone, and you think you hit it off."

"Where was I that night?" Ivy interrupted.

"You were in Richland."

"That's right! You did mention that! Go on, Cleo." Ivy said with forged skepticism.

"Well, we got into an intense discussion on who was the greatest black twentieth-century novelist. I said Richard Wright as opposed to James Baldwin or Ralph Ellison."

Eric nodded, "Yeah, I remember that. You thought there was some psychological impact on Wright's characters as victims rather than Baldwin's or Ellison's."

"So, you two knew each other before we got together," Ivy said, pointing in Eric's direction, then at Cleo.

The room went silent again. Eric glanced at Cleo. They both knew what Ivy was about to say.

"When I introduced you two, you acted like strangers."

"Ivy, you were in love; I couldn't say anything about Eric. Besides, there was nothing between us. We were on campus. It was just about deserted. Almost everybody had gone home. I was lonely, not in love. I think I was stoned out of my mind. We didn't even speak much after that."

"Well, why didn't you tell me you were pregnant with my child?" Eric asked.

"Would it have mattered?"

Eric held his head down as if he probed for an answer that was not readily available.

Ivy almost asked Cleo if she was sure that Tony was Eric's son. Then she remembered the boy she almost ran into that morning - the face and those probing eyes – Eric's. He couldn't deny him, nor could she. Ivy decided to leave that stone unturned. Instead, she asked, "Why did you wait so long? Pausing, she asked, Why now?"

"Ivy, I tried countless times to tell you. I couldn't bring myself to risk our friendship. I left Bowman seventeen and a half years ago. I didn't want to mess up what you two had, either. Believe it or not, I was happy you two got together. I was just ...."

"So why now, like this?" Eric interrupted.

Ivy knew why. "He must be seventeen. Is he a senior this year?"

"He was seventeen on August 9, but he's in his first semester at Morehouse College."

Eric said. "It seems like you've done a good job raising him, Cleo. I only saw him for a quick minute, but I can tell . . . he seems like a nice young man."

"What's his major?" Ivy asked. She couldn't say what was really on her mind. How dare you?

"Philosophy! He wants to teach." I'm sorry about this, Ivy.

"That was my major." Although swollen with pride, Eric held those emotions at bay, waiting for the direction the new development would lead. I'm sorry, Ivy.

"I know." If I could have done it another way, I would have.

"Has he ever asked about his father? Me." Of course, he has. That was a stupid question.

"Always." More than you'll ever know.

"What did you tell him?" Another stupid question.

"I told him the truth. That I had met someone good and honest, but unfortunately, we were not meant to be a couple. I told him one day he would meet his father."

Ivy said with more sarcasm, "When were you planning to do that?" I can't believe this.

"That was my problem. Tony kept asking me when, too! I figured something would work out. This was not the way I hoped it would be." I'm sorry it happened like this!

"Yeah, Cleo, why are we here at this attorney's office anyway? You knew where we lived. You knew everything. Why did you get me to come here like this?"

"Ivy, I'm the senior partner here."

They looked at Cleo in amazement and skepticism, almost not believing what she said.

"Cleo Mitchell, a lawyer? Here? In Evanston? Get out here," Eric said, reluctant to consider the obvious. He remembered the respect she received from the other attorneys. Even the stuffed-up Mr. Scott almost bowed when he left the room.

"I don't practice anymore, but I was a senior partner. Right here. I spend a lot of time in New York these days."

Eric, still somewhat skeptical, asked sarcastically, "Which one are you, Stanley?"

"Yes! Cleo Mitchell Stanley."

Ivy saw some of the old Cleo arise. The quick exchange between the two of them was also reminiscent. "Eric, let her finish!"

Cleo continued. "When I left Bowman, I went to live with Mary."

"Mary? Was she the counselor you talked about?" Ivy interrupted. It was justified that she could. It was her meeting - her party of sorts. She had the right, she thought.

"Yes! She was the only one I could tell."

Mary had consoled Cleo before and after Bowman. They maintained a close relationship that became stronger when Cleo returned to New York. She had been Cleo's bond to the past and her means to the future. In her mid-forties, this soft-spoken, small, gentle woman never married and didn't think it was her purpose. She dedicated her life to taking care of others until the day she died.

Tired was showing hard on Cleo. She was anxious to finish her mission. "Mary took me in and helped me through everything."

Rather than work at a job that prohibited her from spending as much time as possible with Tony, Cleo took on a part-time position at Wells Publishing Company as a reader. She attended classes in the mornings, read manuscripts to Tony at night during dinner, and studied after he went to sleep. Tony was generally a quiet child that tended to be inquisitive. He was handsome, bright-eyed, and seemed much older. He began walking at seven and a half months old and was talking in complete sentences at two. At three years old, he was attending kindergarten full time. Moreover, at just turned five, he was entering first grade.

"It was tough, but I was determined." Cleo continued. "After receiving my B.A. and M.A., I went on to law school. I got a job at the law firm in Manhattan. And here we are."

"Cleo, you've done well for yourself. There's no doubt about that. But how did you get to own this law firm? Down here in Evanston?" Ivy asked.

"I married it. I lived here in Evanston for ten years. My husband was Marvin R. Stanley."

"Marvin Stanley? He was one of the attorneys killed in the plane crash with Congressman Nyland?"

"Yes. That was six years ago."

"Oh, Cleo, I'm so sorry." Ivy's comfort was more for her benefit than Cleo's was. She felt guilty. Ivy thought about all the misfortune that had moved in on Cleo. She thought about how hard times are supposed to make you strong and how weak she must be because her life was, overall, calm and unassuming. Except for the death of her daddy, Ivy had experienced no major tragedy. Big Ma had died two years ago, but she was an eighty-year-old woman who died peacefully in her sleep. Aunt Helen had suffered just briefly from the throes of breast cancer before dying.

Ivy had a loving family all her life, yet she complained. On the other side was Cleo, who had experienced every loss imaginable. She grew up without her mother and father. She lost her brother and her husband and her counselor, Mary. And because she made what she considered a detrimental mistake, she lost her best friend, too.

"Cleo, Lord knows, I'm confused and happy to see you at the same time, but why did you have me come here. We could have done this in private at my home."

"I need you all to be Tony's family."

Eric intruded, "We'll always be Tony's family and yours, too. That's a given. He'll meet Erica and Nikki, and he's welcome in our home whenever he wants. Have you told him about Erica and Nikki?"

"Not yet, but listen, Eric, I have ..."

Eric interrupted again, knowing Cleo's next words would be an unpleasant declaration. Not so much for himself, but he wanted to spare Ivy. He didn't know how much time Cleo had left, but the time she had, he wanted to compress a lifetime of celebrations. He felt a tie to the woman he had a brief encounter with eighteen years ago. Not only would it bind him, but all of them together. Forever. "Cleo, you said yourself that Tony wanted to know who I was. Now he'll know me. He'll know his two sisters and a whole lot of other family members that he needs to know. Besides, the girls have always wanted a brother. All of us can make up for all this lost time. And you and Ivy got a lifetime to make up. Look, you're a part of the family, too."

Ivy wanted to restrain Eric's tangent, but she couldn't. If she let him continue to babble on about his plans, somehow, the inevitable would cease to be a reality. She could pick up where they left off years before... like one of the card games at the Dungeon. When someone left the table for a few minutes to dance or go to the bathroom, you placed your cards on the table, faces down, and enjoyed the party until the other players returned.

"We can start today, now – we've wasted too much time already," Eric concluded as he looked at Ivy for her approval.

Cleo knew the malignancy consuming parts of her body had also eaten away parts of her spirit. None of her money would change fate. She had come to terms with that.

Tony entered the boardroom. All eyes greeted him, and Ivy was relieved. His entrance put an end to Eric's proclamation – his spirited decree. What he said was noble, but Ivy thought it was excessive - almost forged. He was trying to redeem himself, but he had nothing to save. It happened. All he could do was start anew. Now. That day.

"Is everything alright, Momma?" Tony asked as he walked over to Cleo and sat next to her.

"Yes, dear, everything is fine." She took his hand, lightly patting it.

Even though he felt all the awkwardness of the moment, Eric stood, walked over to Tony with extended hands, "Hello, son. I'm your father, Eric Brennan." As tears formed in their eyes, father and son spoke no other words, and those warm extended hands turned into a full embrace.

Ivy and Cleo exchanged glances of approval. What impact would this day have on their lives? Ivy thought of Erica and Nikki and how they would handle the news of a new brother. She thought of Cleo and Tony and wondered how much time they had left together. She thought of the guilt that Eric must feel for missing so much of Tony's life. Then she remembered a song her daddy sang at Second Baptist Church years ago:

Blest be the tie that binds our hearts in Christian love;
The fellowship of kindred minds is like to that above.
Before our Father's throne we pour our ardent prayers;
Our fears, our hopes, our aims are one,
Our comforts and our cares.
We share each other's woes, our mutual burdens bear;
And often for each other flows the sympathizing tear.

When we asunder part, it gives us inward pain;
But we shall still be joined in heart,
And hope to meet again.
This glorious hope revives our courage by the way;
While each in expectation lives,
And longs to see the day.
From sorrow, toil and pain, and sin, we shall be free,
And perfect love and friendship reign through all eternity.

The business was done for the day, at least. It was twenty minutes to three. Erica and Nikki would be getting out of school soon. Ivy remembered that she had forgotten to call Moseley.

"Oh well," she said as she walked to the door of the chilly boardroom. With a tight grip on the doorknob, she looked back over her shoulder at Eric, Cleo, and Tony. Calmly, she said, "Let's go home. It's been a long day."

As they left the boardroom, Ivy retrieved the file that Mr. Scott had earlier guarded so securely. She opened it and gaped at the cashier's check:

Pay on demand to Ivy B. Brennan, the Sum of Two Million and 00/100 Dollars.

Part II

Cleo's Song

Prologue

Thursday had begun ordinary, but by afternoon normality had ended with no chance of compromise. Inevitability had brought them to the point of no return. Life, as it was hours earlier, had become time past. Indeed, the business was done for the day. However, there was a business of a special kind to be handled. A business that needed addressing in a manner unlike before. The sort of business that would define who they all were.

It seemed like a dream. As if the day had not happened at all. The meeting, I mean. My head was still spinning. Absorbing. The meager drive from Evanston back home to Lawrenceville seemed much longer than it did going. The clouds had assembled in the sky and turned a dark shade of gray. Then the raindrops came. Slow and methodical. They looked as if they were dancing down the windshield of my old car. I had just noticed how old my car really was - the sun faded dashboard and worn-out seats. The dings and chipped paint at the rear passenger side where I had backed into the garage door. That had been years ago.

The wipers were clapping at this rain that came down leisurely. Then it came fast - pouring at times. I imagined they were applauding the performance of the unexpected raindrops. Then again, were the raindrops actually tears brought on from the day's unexpected events?

~ *Ivy*

Reckoning

Cleo sat quiet and still in the black limousine that followed a close distance behind Ivy's car. The driver peered through the rearview mirror to the glass opening that separated them. "Is everything alright, Mrs. Stanley?" He asked.

Cleo didn't know if everything was alright, so she didn't answer. The reunion of the day played fresh in her mind, and she delighted in the mild exuberance she had seen in Ivy. How different she'd seemed. A difference that comes with blessings and age, like paying your dues young and reaping the treasures in adulthood. All while they had experienced different lives, Cleo had long realized that someday she and Ivy would have to tie their past to the present that had now slipped upon them.

Reclining in the refinement of the limousine, thoughts of the day crowded her mind, and she didn't know what to feel. Weary and bewildered, Cleo dozed off to sleep. Soon, flashes of lightning, followed by loud thunder, broke the calm. The driver swerved the steering wheel sharply, causing the car to run off the rain-soaked highway - blowing a tire. "Are you alright, Mrs. Stanley?" The driver shouted, still gripping the steering wheel with both hands.

"What the...," Cleo cried out. Startled at first, then angry that there would be a delay.

"Yes, I'm okay."

Through the rearview mirror, Ivy saw the limousine halfway on the low shoulder of the highway – the other half disturbing the flow of traffic. She had to turn around. A momentary lapse in judgment caused Ivy to slam on breaks, place her car in reverse, and back up a quarter mile down the highway's emergency lane. Although the rain had slowed to a trickle, the cars and big trucks bullying down the road made Ivy's car shake all the way to the limo. She carefully got out of the vehicle on the passenger side, sliding down the embankment. With mud-splattered clothes and soaked shoes, Ivy made her way to the limousine.

"Are you guys alright?"

"Flat tire. I'm calling the service. They'll send another car. It'll be about thirty minutes, though," the limo driver said as he held the phone, trying to reassure Cleo.

"Cleo can ride with me," Ivy said. "No need for both of you to wait, right?

Cleo's Song

The driver nodded in agreement while helping Cleo out of the unsteady vehicle. "I'll come behind when the other car gets here."

The reality of the recent revelation at the law office of Stanley, Genwright, and Murray had taken on a manner of urgency. They both knew what they needed to do and what they needed to do had nothing to do with either of them. Their feelings and any unspent emotion had to be recessed for the good of the children. For now, anyway.

Up until then, Ivy hadn't considered how she would break this unexpected news to Erica and Nikki. Neither had she thought about their reaction. For fourteen years, Erica had been the oldest; the one who would go to college first; the one who would make her Daddy proud. There were other people to consider, too. Not that she feared a hostile response from her family, but still all had to be considered. Iris, Michael, and Anthony Darnell? How would they react to her new . . . New what? What would Tony be to her, anyway? He wasn't her son. He was her husband's child. He couldn't be her son because he had a mother already. Stepmother? Not even that. Besides, stepson sounded so unloving to her. And what would he call her?

She thought of Eric's family. What would they think? Mama Hattie and the other kinfolk - they were a strange lot. Geechee people, she called them. Although they were black folks from South Carolina (same as her family), they were different, at least to her. The way they talked, the foods they ate. Even the way they worshipped was different. Shouting, hollering, falling back, and speaking in tongues. Not that it was bad, just unlike what she was used to. All kinds of thoughts ran around inside her head.

Similar thoughts overtook Cleo, but her worse fear wasn't folks' reaction to the revelation. But like most mothers, she dreaded the thought of leaving her child. Cleo had never been a praying woman, but she had prayed to God to let her live long enough to see Tony graduate from high school. Now she was asking for college. What next, Cleo – his marriage, and then the birth of his firstborn son? Then what? Before today, she was, although reluctant, prepared to accept the grim reaper's invitation. However, today, a new movie was beginning, and she wanted to watch it until the credits rolled. She remembered Dylan Thomas' poem and vowed not to go gentle into that goodnight. She would kick and scream in the dying of the light.

"Cleo, what in the world are we going to do?"

She heard Ivy's voice echoing from a distant place and woke from the menacing tirade going on inside her. "I don't know."

Small Talk

The ride home for Eric and Tony was quiet and calm. They had an occasion or two to break the silence, but it was, more or less, a general conversation like, *what did you think about that game Monday night,* followed by *who do you think will make it to the Super Bowl.* The kind of chatter that didn't carry any weight and wasn't supposed to. They were uncomfortable, they knew it, and with that, they felt all right with the quiet. Nevertheless, Eric wondered what Tony thought of him.

Ivy had already pulled into the driveway when Eric and Tony arrived. "You made good time," she said.

Considering the detour to Evanston College to pick up Eric's car, he and Tony had made good time getting back to Lawrenceville. A blue-suited attorney from the law firm had dropped them off. Tony had noticed the campus and thought for a second about transferring. He quickly refuted the notion. He liked Atlanta too much. Morehouse College was a good fit for him.

He could have gone to any school. But he picked that one. Cleo had tried to sway his attention to one of the northern Ivy League universities. With his grades and her money, there would have been no problems with his acceptance to Brown or even Harvard. However, Cleo suspected that he had followed some girl down south. He later admitted he did. He broke up with the girl soon after but decided he liked Atlanta anyway. Cleo left him alone.

"Yeah, I guess we did make good time," Eric responded half-heartedly. He paid no attention to the garage door that was stuck halfway open. Again. He had intended to fix it.

They all had dark thoughts on how the next scene would play out. Eric's 'expect the unexpected' approach was, somehow, inappropriate. He needed a firm grasp of the situation at hand. One imprecision of words or actions could throw us in irreparable turmoil, he thought.

"Well, let's go on inside." Ivy's hesitancy showed. No doubt, she wanted Eric there for the disclosure, but she couldn't see how Cleo and Tony's presence could be beneficial.

Cleo observed their distress. "Maybe we should let you talk to the girls first. We can go to a hotel." But she couldn't leave, not now. Things were still incomplete. Something had to be done. She'd come too far.

Cleo's Song

The trap door hadn't fallen, and maybe there was a way out, Eric thought. If he could have a few days to ease the news on the girls, the whole thing could work out. "That may be a good idea," he said without looking at them.

Eric is scared. Ivy thought how her big, strong protector could fear anything. The strong vanquisher of a few hours ago had been reduced to a mere man. Was he ashamed of his past foolishness? Did he think the girls would lose respect for him; stop loving him? Well, his feelings were not the issue. As much as she didn't want to admit it, the girls' feelings were not the issue, either. Time was the issue. They had come this far.

No, we need to do this thing now. "The same issue will be here tomorrow and the day after," Ivy said. "Come on. Let's go inside before the storm comes."

Cold Pizza

There was an air about Cleo. She exuded class and sophistication, at least on the surface. Her limousine, designer clothes, shoes, and Fendi bag told the story of a woman of influence. Ivy wondered how many years it had been since Cleo had eaten cold pizza from a box. With all of her possessions and great connections, she seemed at home in the ordinary surroundings of the Brennan kitchen, sitting in an oak captain's chair at a round oak table that rocked just a little when leaned on. Night had surfaced, and the mere introduction of Cleo to the girls as "My best friend from college, and this is her son, Tony," had been sufficient, temporarily.

The moon and stars hid behind a cloudy sky that cast no light. The pitch-black night held a strange likeness to the three people who sat at the round oak table, talking about the good old days while avoiding the now. The tiredness that held Cleo earlier in the day had returned, but she fought hard to contain it.

Cleo's Song

It had been a long while since Cleo relaxed. Her life was filled with people who catered to her for what she had, not because of who she was. Not many knew Cleo Mitchell, the unfortunate girl from Brooklyn whose mother had left them and was later found dead – 'cause unknown'. Cleo had been lonely with those people who didn't know her. With Ivy, she wanted to savor the moments.

"What's up with you two?" Nikki asked in a cheerful mood while she walked from the living room, where she had been entertaining Tony with stories about school, the neighborhood, and the family.

"Nothing's up with us. What's up with you all?" Eric tried to make light with his response. Instead, it came out forced and fake. He knew it.

Ivy pretended she didn't notice. "You want more pizza, Nikki?"

"No, thanks, but Tony wants another slice of pepperoni," Nikki answered.

"Here, take this piece." Eric lifted the untouched pizza from his plate and placed it on a clean one. It was cold.

"You need to heat it in the microwave, Nikki," Ivy said.

"No...the microwave makes it too chewy. It's better cold."

"Where's your sister?"

"She's yapping on the phone with some boy."

Eric shouted in a tone that was louder than he had intended, "Tell her to get off the phone right now."

"Stop yelling, Eric. My head is throbbing," Ivy said. "Nikki, tell your sister to come here.

"Okay. Can we watch a movie later?"

"Yes, you may," Ivy said, smiling. Nikki's naïveté made Ivy question how she would receive the revelation about Tony. In truth, Nikki wasn't naïve. Just kind-hearted.

"The VCR is in your room."

"I'll bring it down," Eric said.

"Nikki, tell Tony I need him to help me unhook the VCR and tell your sister I said to hang up that phone. Now!"

"Why can't I help?" Nikki asked.

"You can help." Eric's voice calmed as he felt tension on the horizon.

Nikki was his helper. Whenever there was a project to be done, it was Nikki there with the toolbox or the glue to help Eric either patch up or mess up. She was his Spades partner, bowling partner, and his buddy. Now he found himself in the awkward position of betraying his apprentice while at the same time slighting Tony.

"Ivy, you need another VCR," Cleo said.

"Girl, we got two, Ivy said, laughing so hard she spilled Coke on her suit jacket. "A tape is stuck in the other one, and you-know-who can't get it out."

"Why not buy another one?"
"We're getting the girls one for Christmas."
"Why wait?"
"We don't have it going on like that."
Cleo laughed. "Did you get that file from the office?"
"What file?" *Ivy thought, how could I forget that?* She rushed to the dining room table and pulled a brown folder from her briefcase. Inside was the file Mr. Scott had given Ivy earlier that day. The check worth more than any she'd ever written - or seen – was on top...
Pay on demand to Ivy B. Brennan, the Sum of Two Million and No/100 dollars.
Ivy screamed out loud. "Is this the real thing?"
"As real as us. It's a cashier's check."
"But, what for?"
"For you."
"You mean to tell me that I can take this to a bank and get two million dollars."
"All day long."
"But why?" Ivy stood in disbelief, still gazing at the grainy green piece of paper.
"Why do you keep asking me these questions, Ivy? It's legitimate."
"Nobody gives away two million dollars, Cleo," Ivy screamed louder.

"What is the matter with you, Ivy?" Eric asked as he walked into the kitchen where the women were enjoying each other's company.

"Nothing." She hesitated, "What's wrong with you?" She smiled.

Shaking his head, Eric said, "There's a tape stuck inside our VCR, too. Hand me a butter knife, will you?"

Ivy looked like a fox caught with the hen in his mouth. She passed him the knife from her plate. Tomato sauce and cheese covered it.

"Ivy, what am I going to do with this dirty knife? What's the matter with you?" Eric knew something had changed since he'd left the kitchen.

"Nothing. Come over here." She patted the chair. "Sit down."

"What's up, Baby? I'm trying to fix this thing for the kids."

"I want to show you something." Ivy figured she'd prolong him wrecking the VCR as long as she could. He had tried to fix the girls' VCR when a tape had lodged in it. Although he was able to save the tape, the VCR never worked again.

Cleo held her head down as if reading the Jet magazine that lay on the table with the rest of the day's mail of sales flyers from local stores.

"What is it you want to show me, Honey?"

"Just come here. Please."

"The kids . . ."

"They'll wait. Come here."

Ivy held the check up to her forehead like she had the winning card in a bid whist game.

"What's that?" He asked while squinting his eyes to read the piece of paper.

"It's a check."

"I see that. What is it for?"

"For us. Did you see how much?"

Eric bent down to read the paper that had fell from Ivy's head onto the table. "That's not real."

"Yes, it is. Why don't you ask Cleo?" Ivy was disappointed that she didn't get the response she thought she would.

Eric picked up the check and handled it for a few seconds. He turned it over. It looked like the real thing. "What's up with this, Cleo?"

"It's a cashier's check," Cleo said without looking up.

"We can't take this," he said, half believing the check was real. He tossed it back on the table. The idea that they might be millionaires was ludicrous. "We can't take this." The second time was to convince him.

Ivy didn't speak, but her mouth flung open as if she wanted to.

"Look, Eric," Cleo whispered. "I'm giving this money to all of you. I have to. With what I've asked you and Ivy to do for ...."

"Why would you even think that we would accept that kind of money from you, Cleo?" Eric was less annoyed than he sounded, yet more uncomfortable than he looked.

"And why not?" Her voice was elevating with every word. "I have more money than I can spend. Tony is well taken care of and who can't use money."

"Forget it," Eric shouted. He raised the check from the table to view the evidence of his failure and tossed it down, again." With an awkward laugh, he finished his last word before leaving the room, "I don't think we need any charity just yet."

Ivy didn't know exactly what Eric felt when he saw the check, but she did know it wasn't poor. *He earns a good living. A professor's pay may not be as much as a lawyer's salary, but hell, my husband does honorable work every day and barring a big lottery win or some other miracle; he will never have two million dollars. Besides, I work, too. Together we make ends meet, and we can put money aside for the girls' education. Who does Cleo think she is?*

Eric headed up the steps as Ivy reclaimed the check from the table and followed close behind him. She stuck it in the dresser drawer beneath her underwear and other delicates – the same place she'd kept the money Iris had sent her when hard times came – where she believed Eric wouldn't dare look. But he did.

Cleo's Song

Cleo's apology didn't come easy. Nor did she feel ashamed to share her wealth. She did have more money than she needed. The law offices in New York, Baltimore, and Evanston were doing well financially. Wall Street had been good to Marvin Stanley before and after their marriage. An apartment overlooking Madison Avenue, the homes on Hilton Head Island in the winter and Martha's Vineyard in the summer, and the Charlestonian in Evanston that she refused to live in after Marvin died were worth well over two million dollars.

The exhaustion she had suppressed suddenly caught up to her. Her body weakened as she tried to stand. She leaned on the table for support. Still, her knees buckled. The pressure from her weight caused the table to tilt, sending her and its contents crashing to the floor.

Tony rushed to the kitchen. He kneeled down and lifted Cleo's head, crying out, "Mama!"

Eric, Ivy, and the girls followed close behind. Ivy moved quickly to the floor beside Tony. "Check her pulse," she yelled.

Tony thought he would know what to do if something like this happened. He had prepared for it...in his head. Now he knew the reality of never being prepared enough. "Help me get her up, Daddy," Tony shouted. "Help me, please."

Cleo opened her eyes, almost embarrassed she had caused the disruption. "I'm okay," she mumbled. Although everyone in the household felt relieved that Cleo was 'okay,' there was something else that had presented itself that was not 'okay.' At least not then. No other words were spoken. Not yet. Just an apologetic sigh from Eric.

Then the words came like a brisk rush of a cold Michigan winter. "Damn!" Eric cried, holding his head in his hands, "I'm so sorry."

Ivy knew those words were meant for all of them…individually and together, so all she could do was cry, too.

Six o'clock

Yesterday had been host to a noble confession. It had been a moment of discovery and necessary disclosure. The assurance of time and temperament had forced the day of reckoning.

Friday morning peaked in faintly through the mini blinds. Cleo lingered in bed in a halfway sort of sleep, the kind of sleep that makes you aware, but your dream still hangs on. It was quiet, but the silence played robustly in her mind. She reflected on the day before. There was neither sorrow nor remorse but an uneasiness that dwelled inside her. She had finally released the heavy lump that had lain silent in her throat for nearly half her life. There was still that affecting question, the one that prohibits conclusiveness. Where do we go from here?

"Cleo! Are you awake?" a small voice asked as the door to the bedroom opened and startled her awake fully.

"Yes! I'm awake." Cleo said as she pushed herself up on the plump pillows that surrounded her in the strange bed. She looked around the room for some semblance of familiarity. It was smaller than the ones she had grown accustomed to. Not like the ones in the penthouse on Madison Avenue, where the elite slept with disquiet. Or the beach house on the Atlantic near Hilton Head Island, where the waves pound hard on the large dock a mere foot from outside her bedroom window.

Nevertheless, this room, though tiny in comparison to what she was used to, was neat, orderly, and, most of all, comforting. The bed was small and stood pushed up against a white wall of pastel unicorn pictures and posters. The furnishings were scarcely there but were a perfect fit. Cleo didn't remember going to bed. Except for her clothes strewn across a white wicker chair, everything in the room was new to her.

"How are you feeling this morning?" The voice entered the bedroom, slowly making its way to where Cleo was propping herself up on her elbows.

"I'm okay," Cleo said, unsure if she meant it.

"That's good."

"What time is it?" Cleo inquired of the shadow that had sat at the foot of the bed. She felt the matted wig resting on her head and fluffed it out the best she could.

"Six o'clock. Friday morning."

Cleo's Song

Cleo reached for the lamp that sat on the night table. Before she could make contact, the shadow had clapped twice. Out of the dimness emerged a pajama-clad girl with an innocent smile. "Good morning, young lady."

"Hello," Nikki whispered as if she had more to say but was unable to manipulate the words from her mouth.

"I think I passed out. I don't remember coming in here or putting on these bedclothes."

"Yeah, I know. Daddy and Tony brought you in here. Me and mama helped you get dressed for bed. You don't remember any of that?"

"Yes, vaguely. I think." Cleo felt the sting from the bruise on her arm. It had turned a purplish-black color.

"Miss Cleo, can I ask you something?"

Cleo wondered what the child wanted to ask her at 6:00 in the morning. Out of curiosity, she said, "Yes, sure. What do you want to ask me?"

Nikki stood. "Okay, here goes." She wanted to look mature. Her parents had told her to stay out of grown folks' business, but in her young mind, this was her business. Her daddy was her business would be her defense. "Were you and my daddy married before?"

Cleo gagged and coughed, throwing up a little of last night's cold pizza in her mouth. Nikki reached on the night table and handed her a Kleenex tissue and the glass of water Ivy had placed there the night before. She sat up on the side of the bed, with the morning huskiness still in her voice, "Excuse me."

"You and Daddy...were you married?"

Still gasping, she took another sip of water.

"No, why did you ask me that?"

"Tony!"

"I'm sorry, what?"

"My dad is Tony's dad, right?"

"Right...what?"

"Well, were you all married? I mean before Momma and Daddy?"

"No... but...why?" Cleo thought how different she was from Tony at that age, then she thought again. They were exactly alike. If Tony had something on his mind, he would confront her head-on and point-blank. But she was used to Tony. She didn't know this inquisitive little person who had awakened her.

"You and my daddy had Tony, right?"

"Where's your mom?" Although she thought Nikki was interesting and someone she'd like to know better, at this point, however, Cleo wanted to change the conversation to something other than one in progress.

"Sleep. You want me to wake her up?"

"No. Are you going to school?"

"Yes. How . . ."

Before the next round of interrogation could complete its start, the door to the room swung open.

Cleo's Song

"Good morning, Mama, Tony said, halfway smiling, unsure of what to expect. "Feeling alright?"

"Better than last night, Tony. How did you sleep?"

"Like a baby. Once my head hit the pillow, I was out like a light."

Cleo laughed. "I'm glad."

"What's up, Nikki?" Tony asked.

"Good morning," Nikki responded with indifference. Her mission had been interrupted, so she exited the bedroom, closing the door softly behind her.

"You bout scared the crap out of me last night, Mama."

Cleo laughed. "Sorry, Hon. Bring me my bag. I need to call Dr. Barnard."

"I called him last night. I told him what happened."

"What did he say?" Cleo asked, knowing she should have called him before she left New York. It had been days since her last round of chemo. The medicine is out of me now, she thought.

"He wanted to know what you were doing down here in South Carolina."

"What did you tell him? "

"I told him you were here on business."

"Why on earth did you tell him that?" Cleo was more disgusted with herself than Tony. She had thought she could fly in and fly out, and all this could be over in one day.

"Mama, why didn't you want to go to the hospital last night?" Tony had seen her at her worst before, but this time was different for him. New things were happening, and his young mind couldn't process all the changes.

"Tony, I was tired. That's all. I didn't need to go to the hospital."

"Dr. Barnard was kind of upset with you. He wants to see you in New York. Today!"

"Well, that's not going to happen. I'm not going back right now. Not until I finish this. I don't want to leave this world with you by yourself."

He interrupted, "Mama, I'm not by myself. We have friends in New York."

"Just because folks are friendly towards you don't make them your friends. Sure, we know people - the partners in the firm, the people at the club. I even have friends in Congress." She continued, "But, I wouldn't trust one of them with making sure you're taken care of when I leave this world. The only person I would consider, other than Ivy and Eric, is Victor Moseley, and he's so old. I expected him to kick the bucket before me, anyway."

"Mama, you know that's so wrong on so many levels," Tony said, laughing.

"Yeah, but it's the truth. I know the man is every bit of ninety years old if he's a day."

"You wrong for that!" Tony laughed harder. "But seriously. When are we going to talk about the transplant? I'm seventeen now. Dr. Barnard said...."

Cleo interrupted, "Forget what Dr. Barnard said. I won't let you. Just enjoy your young years. I'm good."

Forceful yet respectful, he said, "Look, Mama, I can do this. You know I can. Haven't I been taking care of you?"

Disregarding Tony's attempt to show his strength, Cleo cheerfully asked, "How did the girls take the news about you last night? Nikki asked me a few pointed questions this morning, so I guess it's all out." Cleo was famous for rearranging the conversation - getting you to talk about another topic of interest so she could table the first.

"Honestly? Nikki was okay, but Erica went off the deep end. She cried and ran up to her room and locked the door. I tried to talk to her, but she ...."

"She didn't take it too well, huh?"

"Naw." He said, scratching his head. "Oh, Mr. Scott called last night, too. He was sending Delaney over to pick me up, but I told him I was staying. He asked how you were."

Tony shifted his position on the edge of the bed. "You know, it's something about that dude I don't like. Ever since I was a little kid, he . . . I don't know."

"Tony, don't pay no mind to Mr. Scott. He's just one of those black people who had a lot of money when the rest of us had a little. He's what we used to call a Negro Aristocrat." She laughed because she was one too.

"I still don't trust him," Tony firmly reiterated.

As Tony left the bedroom, Ivy met him at the door with a high-five and a wink, "Is your mom awake?"

"Yes, she is. And being her usual self. Talking about people."

They laughed. Ivy knew Cleo, and if she was talking trash, she was feeling better.

"Good morning, Ivy."

"Morning. You know you scared the mess out of us last night. Are you all right? You were talking out your head, saying something about Marvin's deposition. When the ambulance came, you cursed those poor guys out. They asked me if you were drunk."

Cleo laughed. "I was tired, Ivy. Besides, I'm tired of the hospital, tired of the doctors. I'm just plain tired."

"What's up with you?"

Cleo hesitated. "Have you heard of CML?"

"No. What's that?"

"It's cancer. Chronic Myeloid Leukemia. I'd been in remission for five years until about two months ago."

The admission fell like a jackhammer on Ivy. She figured cancer had hold of Cleo, but she didn't want to consider that awful truth. At the same time, she had no words of comfort. She wondered why people clamp up when they hear the word cancer. And she was doing the same thing.

"I got some great doctors," Cleo said, trying to reassure Ivy. "I've been on a couple of drug regimens. We'll see if this round of chemo got it by the balls this time."

Ivy knew the best doctors aren't always the answer. She thought about some people who had the best doctors but still didn't make it through.

"Miss Gloom and Doom. I'll be all right. Dr. Barnard is still looking for a compatible bone marrow donor. I've had a couple of donors, but the tissues didn't match. Tony wants to do it, but he's too young to go through that kind of trauma."

Ivy held her head down. She was ashamed for not volunteering, but she knew she couldn't. Chronic anemics couldn't even donate a pint of blood, let alone bone marrow.

"People do survive cancer, you know. But, just in case, Tony needed to know his Daddy."

"You talk like you're not even scared, Cleo."

"I'm scared." Cleo fell back on the pillows. "Believe me. I'm as scared as hell. But I have to act like I'm not."

Ivy hugged her friend. A tear fell from the corner of her eye and rolled slowly down her face. She was scared, too.

Willie Walker

For weeks, Cleo and Ivy had anticipated the journey to the city. It would be their only chance to see the Isley Brothers live in concert before the semester ended. Late February and not the ideal time to travel to Asheville, North Carolina, almost two hours away from Bowman College. Although unusually warm, Interstate-40 remained wet from the thawing snow of a recent winter blizzard. Eric's Volkswagen Beetle made its way up and down the winding mountain road as the tall pine trees waved at them passing by. Intermittent tunes of Al Green, the Isleys, and Rufus blasted from the eight-track player, and Ivy daydreamed of being Chaka Khan while humming off-keyed melodies in the front seat. Cleo sat in the tiny back seat with Willie Walker, half annoyed and halfway enjoying the snow scenes that halfway reminded her of home.

That trip was supposed to have been for Cleo and Ivy. Just a girls' night out. Eric, however, had already purchased two tickets for the concert when Ivy told him

Cleo's Song

she had made plans to go with Cleo. He'd said he would ask his friend to come along, and they'd make it a double. *The nerve of him.* Cleo thought, *Imposing on our plans.* She had contemplated the situation and concluded that Ivy was on her shitlist but later removed her from it when she realized they wouldn't have to pay for food and gas. Cleo found it was a fair compromise.

"Are you guys alright back there?" Ivy had asked more than once. She'd sensed frustration from Cleo but wasn't sure of the reason.

"Yeah, sure," Cleo answered. "My foot just went to sleep." She unzipped her boot and flexed her foot up and down, rubbing it to get the feeling back.

"Here, let me rub it," Willie said.

"Never mind, Romeo. I can do it by myself."

He lifted his arms to stretch while mimicking a yawn. When his arms landed, one was around Cleo's neck, the other rested gently on her thigh.

"What's your problem, fool?" She elbowed him hard in the ribs.

"Aah, girl," he moaned. That hurt like hell."

"Well, move over, or the next one won't be that high," Cleo mumbled through clenched teeth.

"What's going on back there?" Eric asked the question, but he already knew the answer. He knew Willie. Eric positioned the rearview mirror to observe the back seat. Just to keep tabs on Willie and his antics – to keep Ivy off his back, too.

"Your friend is a freak," Cleo replied. "A freak of nature."

"Nah, man. I'm just trying to be friendly, and your girl ain't cooperating."

"You alright, Cleo?" Ivy asked without turning around. She'd seen Cleo handle guys like Willie at the Dungeon. She wasn't worried.

Cleo didn't answer. She could handle the annoyances of unwanted male advances. What she needed was a one-on-one conversation with her best friend. Ivy. The Willie Walkers of the world would always be around, and as long as she had one good knee and a quick left jab, she'd be all right with the Willie Walkers. A good friend was scarce. Ivy had been her best friend, yet lately, Ivy's usual concern for Cleo had been scanty at best. She had academic books to read and more papers to write for challenging professors, but more importantly, she had allowed Eric into her world, and he was getting the lion's share of her attention.

The Asheville Arena was loud, and the crowd was anxious. They had arrived early enough to get prime floor seats. "Thank God and University Promotions for general admission seating," Willie said while leaning back in the metal folding chair next to Cleo.

When the concert kicked off, Cleo was kicking Willie off of her. He rubbed, hugged, and tugged on her as she elbowed, kneed, and slapped him repeatedly.

Then somewhere between the hand-clapping to one band and bouncing to the beat of another, Cleo submitted to Willie's impious pleas. She had succumbed to the joy of the moment. Ivy witnessed with unease Cleo's emerging warmth towards the wicked Willie Walker. She was aware of Willie's sexual exploits, yet her worry was not for that one night of folly but tomorrow. How could Ivy let her friend be Willie's latest conquest? She made a mental note. *We'll talk tomorrow.*

The mood was just right for lovers and others who pretended for love's sake. Eric motioned Ivy to pass him the half-empty quart of Johnny Walker Black Label whiskey she had smuggled in her oversized shoulder bag.

"Eric, don't you think you had enough to drink?" Ivy asked.

"Not yet, but I'm getting there," he said cynically, already high from the joint he'd been smoking.

Willie laughed, "Let me have a hit of that shine, too, man."

Cleo nudged Willie lightly.

"No, man, that's alright. I'm going to sit this one out." Willie pushed the brown bag away.

"Come on, Walker. It's only a corner left. It's got your name on it." Eric laughed.

"Maybe Willie wants his liver," Cleo jumped in.

"And when did you start worrying about a liver, Miss Cleo." Eric's speech slurred as he spat out those chastising words. He was drunker than he thought.

Ivy snatched the brown bag from Eric and stuffed it back in the leather bag. A strange thing had happened to the two people who, hours earlier, couldn't get past 'hello.' Now, Willie clung tight to Cleo like an irregular pair of pantyhose two sizes too small. Through the faultless performances of Rose Royce and the Dazz Band, they had settled on each other like old lovers. Ivy's thoughts muddled over the authenticity of both their actions. She considered interference then thought she'd leave it alone and see if the sun would come up on that damned union.

They almost looked nice together, Ivy admitted. Willie was short for a man, the same height as Cleo with heels. He wore a big Tito Jackson hat and almost looked like him from the side. He wasn't unattractive, but not handsome like Eric, she thought. The problem was not his looks per se but his ways. He had a sordid reputation with the women on campus. That didn't sit well with her, particularly now - while he had her friend in his grasp.

It was past midnight. The Isleys' performance was better than expected, considering the late hour. Cleo and Ivy were popping fingers to the medley of music that had the whole arena on their feet. After listening to all of the songs from the 3+3 album, the audience knew that

Cleo's Song

they had received more than twenty dollars' worth of a good time no matter what happened next. The concert ended with the same vibrant power had it began with, and a finale song that had everyone in the arena up and singing, *"It's your thang do what you wanna do, I can't tell you who to sock it to. It's your thang do what you wanna do. I can't tell you who to sock it to. If you want me to love you . . ."*

    The parking lot was packed full of patrons trying to exit. Frustrated drivers laid on their horns firmly, honking energetically. Eric joined them as they moved slowly, bumper to bumper from the arena. Cleo and Willie lay head-to-head in the back seat of the tiny car that now seemed big enough for the both of them. The bottle of whiskey that Eric drank caught him off guard. He fought hard to keep his eyes open as he swerved from one lane to the other. The low-lying fog that had set in after the rain further impeded his driving.

    "Willie, you have to take the wheel, man. I'm drunker than a skunk."

    "Hell, I'm too high to get behind the wheel, Eric."

    "One of you ladies wanna drive? Eric's plea went unanswered. They were asleep. Cold, snoring sleep or pretending devilishly well.

    "Man, we need to get a room," Willie said.

    "I got eleven dollars to my name, Blood."

    "We'll have to get two double beds 'cause all I have is a twenty."

"That'll work." Eric pulled into a dingy little motel off Interstate-40. "MA_ FLOWER."

It was the Mayflower Motel with one of the neon lights either burnt out or missing.

"We're home already," Ivy asked while reaching down to find the shoes she had kicked off as soon as she got in the car.

Cleo saw the flashing red and white motel sign. "This isn't Bowman. What are you all trying to pull?"

"Nothing!" Willie said. "It's foggy, the roads are icy, and we're too damn drunk to drive."

"Yeah," Eric said, "If one of you ladies wanna take the wheel, be my guest."

Cleo and Ivy engaged in a conversation with their eyes. *I'm not driving. Me either. He better go somewhere. Laughing...straight-faced.*

Ivy wiped the condensation from the front passenger window. "This place is a dive."

"They probably don't change the sheets regular either," Cleo said.

"How can you be sure that any motel change sheets?" Willie added.

His two cents' worth didn't change their minds. "We're not staying here. I hope!"

"We don't have any Holiday Inn money, so I guess this is it," Eric answered calmly.

"I can't believe you came all the way here with no money," Ivy said, folding her arms over crossed legs.

"I had the money. But you had to have a T-shirt and take pictures, and you eat like they don't feed you down in the country."

Ivy was too tired to be annoyed. "Okay, Eric. How much do I owe you?"

Ivy pulled a small, zippered purse from inside her blouse. She had five crisp twenty-dollar bills tucked snugly inside. She handed him one bill.

"Let me know if that's not enough," she said sarcastically and proceeded to pull out another one.

"You don't owe me any money, Baby. But you know my car note is due."

Neither Cleo nor Ivy responded. However, Willie broke the silence. "How do y'all wear them purses down in your blouse without anybody seeing them?"

The Sunday morning sky over Ashville was a clear blue. Mayflower had changed their sheets, after all, and served hot coffee and a continental breakfast, too.

Small flowering trees budding along the perimeter gave the motel some appeal in daylight. Town's folk had shed their winter garb. *It seemed too early for spring,* Cleo thought. An early spring always brings out the best in us. Relief from the throes of winter's despair. However, that year had started unusually. Cleo was about twenty pounds lighter than the day she arrived at Bowman. She hadn't smoked cigarettes or weed since Christmas. And although Cleo and Willie had spent a great night together, they had slept with their clothes and morals intact, and she had aroused a genuine friendship with the notorious Willie Walker.

Reality Speaks Loudly

In the course of life, Cleo had few regrets. She didn't regret her loose ways, for, through her disobedience, she learned self-discipline. Nor did she apologize for bringing a child into a rancid world. Through him, she thought, the world might become palatable. She never lamented over a lost family that was beyond any control she might have had. However, she did regret missing Ivy. That act had been within her power. Now she chose the path that had led her back to where once she found comfort.

Friendships came and went. Some were pleasant enough to soothe, though many were counterfeit. Even her marriage was forged. Though she loved Marvin R. Stanley for who he was to her and her son, he was more of a mentor than the lover she'd yearned for.

Cleo was fresh out of New York University when she met Marvin, thirty years her senior. He recruited her along with ten other bright attorneys who had graduated at the top of their class. He was particularly interested in Cleo. She was feisty and arrogant - an essential characteristic of a great lawyer, he'd said. She became his star attorney, winning simple civil lawsuits to some notable precedent cases. A whirlwind romance led to a New York society wedding and a pretentious honeymoon on France's Left Bank.

She had arrived at the place that she'd brazenly dreamed of but somehow found its reality stale. Her new-found upper crust had satisfied her yearning for status – to be somebody other than that girl whose father died in a prison infirmary. However, she became painfully aware that she had moved to that place where material things sometimes outweighed humanity.

Cleo remembered the last time she saw Ivy. Spring was just beginning. The perfect green grass lay on Bowman College's grounds like new carpet and gently danced in the North Carolina mountain breeze. The smell of a freshly mowed lawn was still fragrant in her mind, and she faintly heard blue jays singing:

"Where are you going this early on Saturday, Cleo?" Ivy *was still in bed. They had made plans to do loads of overdue laundry at noon.*

"Willie invited me to breakfast," she lied.

"Okay, cool. Have fun and hurry back. It's getting funky in here. Phew! My sheets hadn't been changed in a month of Sundays."

"You know I love you, Sis."

"Huh?"

"I love you."

"Back at you. Now hurry back."

Cleo's Song

"Mary," Cleo mumbled in the receiver of the payphone outside of Higgins Hall Dormitory.

"Cleo, What's the matter?"

"What makes you think something is the matter?"

"I've known you long enough to know when you have something on your mind. What's going on?" Mary anxiously inquired.

"But I haven't even said anything," Cleo answered awkwardly.

"I can feel it in your voice, dear. Tell me what's going on. Are you in trouble?"

"Kind of."

"How big of a kind of, Cleo?" Mary asked with a sigh.

"Big!" Cleo said, hoping that would be enough to satisfy Mary's examination.

"Ok. Just tell me."

"It's not easy to talk about over the phone."

"Do I need to come down there?" Mary asked sympathetically.

"No! No!" Cleo answered.

"Well, how do you suggest we talk, sweetheart?" Mary asked.

"I'll come home . . . back to New York if it's okay with you?" Cleo replied with a question.

"Of course! I wondered if you were ever coming back to New York since you didn't come at Christmastime. Spring Break, either."

Cleo said, "I know. I was broke. I didn't want to bother you for money."

"Honey, I'm not rich, but I told you anytime you needed something, all you had to do was ask."

"I know."

"Do you need me to send you plane fare or pick you up?"

"No, I have some money. I'm coming on the dog."

Confused, Mary posed, "The dog? What are you talking about, Cleo?"

"Greyhound!"

"Oh, sorry. I don't know this hip talk you kids speak."

"I'll have to teach you." Cleo laughed with relief that Mary wasn't more interested.

That was Mary. It seemed she was always there when Cleo was in need. Let Cleo tell it, her needing anyone was rare. Yet, theirs was a good kind of female relationship that hung in the middle - between mother and daughter. They had mutual respect and admiration that couldn't be explained by simple words. They knew what they had and what they had was special, like family love, only better. Family love was intuitive. God chooses who's going to be your mother, father, sister, and your brother, without any say-so from you. However, with Cleo and Mary, their tie was spiritual. It was as if God said, I know what you have been through, so I'm putting you two together to make a family. That kind of relationship didn't tend to make one take the other for granted too easily.

The Greyhound bus arrived at the Port Authority Bus Terminal 42nd Street at seven in the morning. It was full of people from all walks of life. Many passengers had started their northern trek from as far south as Miami. Frustration showed on some of the passengers' faces, who still had an even longer ride before their final destinations further north. Cleo wasn't able to sleep. She lamented over seventeen hours, weary at the thought of facing Mary. She wondered how Mary would receive the news she had traveled over seven hundred miles to deliver in person. Cleo pondered the questions. Should I tell her? Where will I go if she doesn't want me back?

She patted her protruding belly over unbuttoned blue jeans as she descended the steps. The other passengers hastily filed past her, some reaching for greeters who warmly embraced them as soon as they met. Her eyes panned the terminal searching for Mary as she waited for her luggage. The fumes from the exhausts of the idling buses made her nauseous. She retrieved the heavy footlocker and rested on it.

Cleo thought of Ivy. *I hate I couldn't tell her I was leaving, but I just couldn't stand the thought of her asking me questions that I couldn't.* Suddenly she felt a thump in the middle of her stomach, and she sighed.

Mary appeared amidst the crowd of passengers who were gathering their luggage. "Cleo, over here!" She made her way through the waiting passengers over to Cleo. "Let me look at you, child?" She grasped Cleo around her shoulders, pulling her to her feet and wrapping her arms around her.

"Hello, Mary." Cleo held her tightly. Mary tried to free herself from Cleo's embrace as she wanted to look at her. However, Cleo held on as if to release the hold would mean losing a moment in time when she felt safe. A backfiring bus startled Cleo, and Mary was freed.

"Cleo, you look good, dear. The south agrees with you."

"Not too agreeable."

"Ah, what are you talking about? Your skin is as smooth as silk, your hair is shiny, and it's grown so long. You look adorable."

Mary tended to adorn the truth to make a person feel special, but in this case, her praise wasn't artificial. Cleo was prettier now. The Afro she had worn eight months earlier had turned into flowing locks of curls that hung to her shoulders. She was slender and looked regal in her studded jean outfit. Although her eyes were bright and sparkling, Mary noticed that they were overshadowed by sadness.

"I'm ready to go to your house. Remind me never to ride that da-. Oops, sorry Mary . . . that darn bus again. It was the longest exhausting ride I ever took."

Cleo's Song

"Cleo, you haven't changed that mouth of yours," Mary said.

"I know," Cleo replied. "I'll do better."

Mary had been alone before Cleo. A single, childless woman, she threw herself into her work to find meaning and purpose. At fifty, she thought she was content with her existence. Then this fifteen-year-old, who some called a hellion, erupted on the scene, full of energy and potential. Out of all the troubled teenagers that had entered the Brooklyn Home for Girls, Mary had yet to meet one who needed someone more. She saw a young girl with a lot of promise in her eyes but no direction in her life. Mary sincerely believed that if you could save one child, then your time on this earth was not in vain. With that attitude and a master's in social work, Mary embarked on her mission to shape Cleopatra Mitchell into the best person she could be.

"What is so crucial that you couldn't tell me over the telephone, Cleo?" Mary asked as they left the terminal.

Cleo ignored the question and instead enjoyed the drive. She daydreamed of the magnificent streets and avenues of Brooklyn and Queens that she missed. Avenues like Jamaica, where she would hang out with her brother, Tony. Fulton Street, where she got her first kiss from one of his friends, who was much older and wanted more. Flatbush, Rockaway, and East New York Avenues, where she shoplifted from the shops that managed to survive there. She noticed the different flavors of the New Yorkers and how no one, other than Mary, had looked at or spoken to her since she arrived.

In the south, if a person had never set eyes on you before, they still greeted you with or without a smile - with a nod of the head or raising of eyebrows. They acknowledged you, even if it was with resentment. In New York, the people looked past you, through you. They could bump into you straight on and disallow your existence. Cleo thought of good and bad reasons for wanting and not wanting to live in the south, or New York, for that matter.

"I guess you'll tell me when you're ready," Mary said in a futile attempt to stir Cleo from her nostalgia.

As they approached the apartment building, Cleo mumbled, "I'm four months pregnant."

"Ok then, I guess I'll have to carry that heavy footlocker up those steps," Mary replied.

August in New York was sweltering. Cleo had gained forty pounds that summer, and she couldn't wait to have that freakin baby. She had said *freakin baby* so much until Mary was fearful it would be born deformed.

"Your hormones are out of whack," Mary said.

At two weeks past her delivery date, Cleo thought, I'm not pregnant after all. I'm just fat with a nine-month-old gas bubble resting on my bladder.

Cleo's Song

Mary rallied all her patience to refrain from throwing Cleo out on the street, temporarily. She resorted to working voluntary overtime so she could be away from Cleo as much as possible. Then one bright and sunny New York morning on August 9 at seven in the morning, Cleo shoved eight pounds and six ounces of joy from her womb; Robert Antonio Mitchell III, after her brother, who was named after her father. He was born smiling with his eyes wide open. Mary said he looked like he had been here before and had just returned to reclaim his place in this world. Whether or not he had been here before was insignificant as Cleo was happy that Tony arrived healthy and was out of her stomach.

It wasn't a full six months after Tony was born when Cleo returned to college. New York University offered her everything she needed - what Bowman College hadn't. Independence. She worked hard at being a student and even harder at motherhood. It was as though she was on a devoutly definable mission, and nothing would fail her. Yet, there were those times when life seemed to push and pull on her like an uncontrollable locomotive - carrying her up one track and down another. She never lost sight of her way. She never derailed.

Days came with exhaustion and went with even more. There were times when Cleo was compelled to lug Tony to class with her, sitting in the back of the large lecture halls, his feet not yet touching the floor and his head barely visible from the seat. He seemed to have enjoyed those times. Cleo often observed him listening attentively during long lectures. He was an icon of sorts. Other students looked forward to his juicy grins and happy garbled chatter. Seven years passed, then Cleo breathed.

Montel Williams?

Friday morning found young Erica in deep despair. You could say she was in mourning. The man who was her 'champion' had slapped her in the face with a testimony of misconduct. An uninviting piece of evidence, Exhibit A, stared at her from across the kitchen table. She dared not look at it. It called itself her brother, but how could Daddy be sure. She remembered Montel Williams and those paternity tests. *This woman who claims to be Mama's friend has some nerve.*

Erica stirred her oatmeal, looking through it. It sat lukewarm and lumpy. An object to keep her eyes away from Tony. She hoped that if she looked up quickly enough, he would disappear like a wanton figment of her imagination. *Momma is not even angry at my daddy. They act like everything's okay. What will my friends think of me with a brother who is not my mother's child but my father's? An older brother at that - I hate all of them. Nikki, sitting over there with her silly self. She's clueless. I hate her, too. Why are they looking at me? I want out of this house.*

"Erica, why aren't you dressed for school," Ivy asked while making her way to the kitchen.

"I'm not going!" Erica lashed out, unwilling to raise an eye.

"And why not?"

"Because I'm not going." She answered rudely.

"Why?" Nikki asked.

Erica ignored her. She thought, *why should you care whether I go to school? No one bothered to ask if I wanted a brother.*

"Nikki, go catch the bus," Ivy said. "Erica will be out in a minute, sweetheart."

Ivy looked around her tiny kitchen. An orange juice jug sat drained on the counter next to strings of dried cheese. Empty pizza boxes and an opened 3-liter Pepsi that went flat in the night sat there, too. She placed both atop the overflowing garbage can, remembering that the Maxwell House Coffee was almost gone. Enough for one pot. *That should be plenty... I'll go to the grocery store on my way to work... Maybe.* Ivy hadn't gone to the grocery store all week. She consciously chose not to go, hoping Eric would notice and volunteer. It was an experiment that had gone awry.

Cleo's Song

Ivy used the last coffee filter. She smelled the sweet, undeniable aroma as soon as the water dripped into the carafe. She remembered that she hadn't called Moseley yet. It was too early to call. He never got in before nine. *He probably knows about everything that happened yesterday anyway.*

The dirty dishes from yesterday had been hastily crammed in the dishwasher. Ivy started the cycle and listened as the machine raucously hummed. She finally sat down. "Child, you better get up from this table and go to school. I'm not feeling your foolishness this morning."

"Mama, I'm not showing my face in school." Erica shoved her words through angry lips.

That's my cue, Tony thought. He raised his tall, lean body from the table before Ivy could ask. He went to the living room. The sheets, pillows, and comforter that had been his bed were shoved into a corner by the front door. He retrieved the oversized pillows from the floor and fluffed the sofa before he sat down.

"Girl, you need to stop tripping and go get dressed. "Ivy said.

"For what?" Nikki snapped back, "Y'all might be all happy 'cause Daddy got this brand-new family, but I'm not."

Tony heard the inflated whispers through the thin walls. He turned on the television to muffle the tension that had seized the downstairs. A different strain of anxiety wallowed upstairs. Cleo lay in bed, flowing in and out of flagrant denial of her condition, while Eric lay awake undecided on what course the recent disclosure would take.

Tony was ready to leave. *Where can I go?* Not knowing a soul in Lawrenceville, *I wish I had my car.* He could drive someplace, anyplace other than the disturbing place where he'd found his father. There was no place to go. He walked out the front door with the notion of hailing a taxi. There were no taxis to hail in Lawrenceville. He sat on the front stoop, contemplating what to do, while the conversation that had once been faint whispers intensified to frantic rants.

"What do you expect me to do? "Ivy asked while attempting to soothe her daughter.

Erica replied with tears rolling down a sad face, "I don't expect you to do a thing, Mama. Not a thing."

"You want me to ask them to leave. Act like he doesn't exist - and all this is a dream that we can wake up from, and life will be like it was yesterday morning? Child, I didn't ask for this any more than you did." Ivy hesitated. She rubbed her temples, hoping that the headache that made its way from the back of her head to her forehead would disappear. It didn't. "It's too late to turn back, Erica. Everything's going to work out. I promise."

"Why all of a sudden, they show up here?" Erica wiped away, freely pouring tears with the back of her

Cleo's Song

hand. Ivy picked up a Pizza Hut napkin someone had placed in the empty napkin holder on the table. She wiped the steady stream from Erica's cheeks. "I guess it was time for them to show up."

"All these years and they show up now. That's stupid. And how do we know he's Daddy's son, anyway? Just because she says so?" Erica didn't want to release that part of her anger, but her heart wouldn't let it remain inside. It was rotten, and it had to come out. Otherwise, she'd throw up.

"Why do you think they would come all the way here and tell us this if it wasn't true?"

"I don't know - you tell me." Erica wiped her nose with a rough paper towel that sat scrunched up on the table. She saw the Pizza Hut napkin, but she refused it just like she had refused Tony. It was unfamiliar to her, and she wanted no part of it.

The noise from the school bus screeching to a halt and starting again impelled Ivy to ask, "I guess that means you won't be catching the bus today."

"I guess not." Erica's smart talk was not too much out of character, yet this newfound rigid discontent surprised Ivy, and she was at a loss for words to comfort her daughter. She knew how to handle Nikki's debates. They had practiced for years. Nikki questioned everything. Ivy was used to that type of exchange. Although the two of them rarely made concessions, they went on, each with her idea. However, Erica had been the steady one. Gentle. Her surroundings never ruffled her. She adapted to whatever the forces presented. Of course, there had been instances when disagreements surfaced, but they were resolved quickly with an appropriate compromise, and life went on – contentedly.

This time was different. People who were not invited had come into their world and rearranged it. The confrontation with Erica left Ivy questioning the complexity of this discovery. Had she been too accepting of the latest exposé?

"Get dressed, Erica. We'll work this out. I promise. Okay?"

Erica didn't respond to her mother with words but slowly made her way up the steps to do as she was told. The aroma of the freshly brewed Maxwell House Coffee was all that remained familiar in the Brennan home Friday morning.

Ivy was comfortable in her belief that Erica would soon come to accept and love Tony. They all would. He was a part of them in blood and in heart on all sides. She no longer worried about what her mother or Eric's mother would think because she knew they would love him, too. That was who they were. A family of love.

A Lesson Before Dying

How can a happy marriage be strained over past events? Events that happened almost twenty years ago. Before the marriage. Before the courtship. Ivy had said, "I will," when asked if she would love Eric for better or for worse. She had seen the better of times. The worse was long overdue.

"Hey, Youngblood." Eric counterfeited a cheerful greeting as he made his way to the kitchen. Nine o'clock. A clichéd *Thank God, it's Friday* entered his mind, and he thanked God it didn't escape his lips. "What's up?"

"Nothing." Tony didn't raise an eye from the book he used to shield his anguish.

Still, Eric's uneasiness was hard to conceal as he fumbled around the dishwasher for his favorite coffee mug. "What are you reading?"

"A Lesson Before Dying."

"How is it?" Eric asked, wondering if there was some hidden meaning behind Tony's curt response.

"It's a pretty good read."

"What is it about?"

"Haven't you read it?" Tony surmised that his father had read it. If he hadn't, he would have lost a little more respect for him.

"Yeah, I read it. Ernest Gaines. It's about a young black man wrongfully accused and convicted of robbing and murdering a white man." Why did Eric feel he had to prove himself? Although last night was awkward, it wasn't strained, he thought. Now Eric was sure. Tony seemed different. But why? He had nothing to reference. Yesterday presented itself hopeful. Although nothing had been constructed, Eric felt that it would have been a matter of time before all disorder would fall into place. He was unsure of what foul incident had occurred between 'good night' and 'good morning.' But he was sure something had caused Tony to reject him like a piece of rotten fish. He wanted to ask what terrible omen had come into his home last night and caused discord. Instead, he clung to the silence that overshadowed the room.

"Whew!" Ivy entered the kitchen from the wet outside. It had started to rain hard again, and the temperature had dipped to cold winter. Ivy wasn't dressed for the sudden change in weather as she threw the drenched umbrella on the floor by the backdoor. Her feet were sockless and soaked in a pair of sneakers. She had dressed quickly, pulling on a sweatshirt and jeans over a sleeveless nightgown. Shivering and cold with clattering teeth, she dropped two full bags of groceries on the kitchen counter.

"Any more groceries in ..." Eric and Tony said at the same time.

Ivy laughed. She hadn't realized how much they were alike until she saw Tony raise himself from the table and pressed the creases of his pants between his fingers. He had inherited Eric's neatness, along with his good looks. She wondered if he ironed his shirts himself, too. She never ironed Eric's clothes. They had to be exactly right – in military order. She wasn't that precise with pressing clothes. If it wasn't wash-and-wear or a light bump of an iron clothing, it went to the Lawrenceville One Hour Dry Cleaners. Then it occurred to her that this kid was rich. He probably doesn't have to iron or do anything for himself. "No! This is all of it," she said while massaging her temples. "I just picked up a few things while I was out dropping Erica off at school."

"She missed the bus?" Eric asked, surprised that Erica had missed riding to school with 'the little *knucklehead* boy from around the corner.'

Ivy emptied two plastic bags that held a container of coffee, deli meats, orange juice, assorted packages of pantry snacks, and Oreo cookies. The Oreos were for Cleo. When they roomed together at Bowman, she remembered Cleo's shameless footlocker stashed with cookies, candies, and marijuana. Cleo had the munchies back then. *She probably hadn't eaten a double stuffed Oreo in years.*

Eric closed the backdoor tight. He felt the brisk chill in the air. "I bet you're used to this kind of weather, Tony."

"Yeah," Tony replied without looking up.

Oh, Lord! What's gone wrong now? Ivy had just defused one unpleasant situation. There wasn't another drop of energy left inside her to neutralize that bomb. Especially one she thought could detonate and blow them all to hell or heaven - whichever one would have them.

"Hey, Tony, how about getting your coat. I need you to ride somewhere with me. Ivy, we'll be back in a little while." Eric didn't allow Tony an opening for refusal. He retrieved two heavy parkers from the hall closet. Tony reluctantly followed Eric as they disappeared out the back door.

"Okay," Ivy said while closing the door behind them. "Take your time." She meant it. A fresh bomb had fallen, but not on her this time. She didn't concern herself with what had come up between them, but whatever had happened would have to be resolved between the two of them. She had enough worry for Erica and Cleo. That was more than enough. Anything else would throw her off balance. They were on their own.

"Cleo. Do you want some breakfast, or are you going to sleep all day?" Ivy called from the stairs. The

Cleo's Song

house had grown colder as the temperature outside continued to drop. Except for the creaking in the stairs, it was mausoleum quiet. The soft raps on the bedroom door didn't seem to disturb Cleo. The ticking of the clock gave the feel of a sluggish heartbeat as she entered the room. Cleo lay still on her side with her body exposed to the chilly room. Ivy slowly moved towards the bed, where her friend lay peacefully.

"Cleo." Ivy nudged her shoulder. Her bare arms were cold like frost. Again, she pushed, but this time forceful. Cleo rolled over on her back, exposing a face that had been drained of color. Her eyes lingered half-opened and half-closed. She wasn't awake, nor was she asleep. Thick saliva mixed with a pinkish substance had traveled down the folds of her mouth and left a crusty patch on her face. Ivy called out louder, "Cleo!"

Time Out

All problems have a resolution. Some of the decisions we make are foolish and adds to our troubles. But Eric was a level-headed and logical-thinking man. He was usually textbook logical when it came to his family. He used reasoning consistently to come to decisions involving Ivy and the girls. He knew that this new situation needed structure, relationships between facts, and a chain of reasoning that made sense. Not just for him but for the family, Cleo and Tony, too. And being the logical thinker that he was, he knew the best solution to this life's challenge was a pick-up game of basketball at the YMCA.

Eric and Tony entered the gym and instantly got in an intense game of ball with a few men who worked second shift at one of the manufacturing plants nearby. Although they were strangers to this group, their height guaranteed them a place on the floor. Fortunately, Eric and Tony landed on the same team.

Cleo's Song

The game started with high energy. A member on the team passed the ball to Eric. He took the first shot, and it landed in the hoop perfectly. The opposing team made a 3-pointer, and Tony got the rebound. As he leaped to take the shot, a rival player slapped it out of bounds. "That's okay, that's okay," Eric yelled.

The rival player took the ball out and passed it to another player. Tony ran up beside him and stole the ball. "Good job, good job, man. Good job. Now lay it up, man, lay it up," Eric yelled.

Tony ignored him, traveling up to the goal, missing the shot.

"Come on, man. Come on, man," Someone shouted.

"It's OK. It's OK," Eric countered.

The game continued with Tony ignoring Eric's help. He missed shots, fouled a couple of players, and hurt his finger, all while trying to be a cracker-jack player to impress an audience that he didn't know and who didn't care to know him. "Timeout." The score was 16 to 18. Not in their team's favor.

On the bench: "Man, let me tell you that these guys are good," one player said. Hey kid, you need to listen to your old man. He's telling you the truth. You got to lay it up before you take a shot. Those cats play tournament ball."

As the game resumed, the team was well-aligned and playing with precision. *Lay-up, Pass, Shoot. Layup,*

Shoot. Two points. Eric and Tony were amazed at each other's skills shooting and guarding the opposition. They learned something about each other that day. Tony was a hothead but willing to listen. Eric had wisdom and patience and gave second chances. The game ended 56 to 54. They had lost the game, but they were loaded with excitement, agreeing to come back again.

The emotional weight of the ride back home was lighter than it was going. They talked more than small talk. Tony opened up to Eric about his concern for his mother. He also admitted that he was afraid Cleo would die soon. Eric gave him comfort in the assurance that he was his son. He admitted he didn't know what to do but was willing to take on any challenge that came with this new role.

Those years between boyhood and manhood are critical. Although he didn't get those years with Tony, Eric applauded Cleo for raising his son to be smart and respectful. Learning to be a young man in middle school and high school was hard for him, even with his large extended family. He could only imagine the anxiety Tony must have endured after his stepfather was killed. But he didn't know, so he let that worry go in the wind.

God's Hands

There had been countless debates between Ivy and Eric on the advantages of living in Lawrenceville instead of Evanston. His argument had been the lack of genuine social interaction with their neighbors that provided for healthy bonding. He had grown up in a neighborhood where corporate responsibility was the norm. Everyone looked after everyone else. He desired that same comfort for his children.

Ivy had countered with finer schools, prestigious shopping malls, better-quality grocery stores, and *more venues for cultural activities and socializing*. Friday morning, she added another benefit to Eric's list - prompt and efficient EMS response.

The Lawrenceville Emergency Medical unit responded within minutes of Ivy's incoherent 9-1-1 call. The same EMS unit that had responded less than twelve hours earlier once again had come to the rescue, this time without thankless abandon. But cohesive and caring. They checked her breathing. It was faint. So was her pulse. "How long has she been unconscious?'

I'm not sure," Ivy said, trying to remember if she had heard Cleo get up after she left the room around 8 o'clock that morning. She was hopeful and said, "About an hour."

They asked other questions, but Ivy didn't know the answers to those either. She felt helpless because she didn't know anything about Cleo's illness other than having cancer. The paramedics prepared the padded stretcher to transport Cleo to the hospital safely. Ivy called Eric's mobile phone, "Meet me at the hospital," she said calmly. There was no need to panic. *It was all in God's hands.*

Ivy's head was still throbbing from the night before, but she couldn't think much about that now. She placed a cold/ wet towel on her head and made another phone call.

Victor Moseley and Cleo had known each other for a long time. He would know what to do, she thought. Although Tony knew of Cleo's illness, how much had she told him? He was a child, albeit bright and mature; he could not process the specifics of it. Not the intimate ones that adults tell each other because of a mutual commonality of having *gone through it.* The ones about

Cleo's Song

life that one would have had to live through. Experienced firsthand in some capacity to know how to winnow the wheat from the chaff. Together, Cleo and Moseley had experienced the emotions that came with this illness, and they made rational decisions. They were able to distinguish between feelings and practicality to choose the best option.

Plastic tubes and cold metal machines connected in the ICU labored while Cleo clung to life in Lawrenceville's small community hospital. Dr. Barnard had informed them of Cleo's medical history. More importantly, they had a perfect stem cell match. The doctors and nurses diligently provided the best care while awaiting the medical helicopter to transport Cleo and the stem cells to Emory University Hospital, over a hundred miles away. Was Cleo well enough to receive the transplant? What was her chance for a full recovery? Remission? Again, *it was all in God's hands.*

Epilogue

That Friday morning had begun extraordinarily, but by afternoon normality had ended with no chance of compromise. Inevitability brought them to a place of no return. Life, as it was hours earlier, became time past.

My friend died. There are no words of comfort that can fill this void. It hurts even worst because I had not seen her for years. Too many years. We were just beginning again. I am aware of the inevitability of death, and yet it still doesn't make sense. I guess the purposeful thing I should remember is that we got to see each other again ....

She hadn't suffered. The doctor told us the ruptured aneurysm caused a massive brain injury from the bleeding, and she went quickly.

The memorial service was beautiful. Still, family and friends could not see that part yet. People attended who I never dreamed I'd see again. The good ones. Friends from Bowman. I smiled, imagining that she was watching us all together again... like we used to be... young and carefree. I mingled with these people who looked different from before – yet I noticed that they hadn't changed at all because the spirit never changes. Always notice the spirit.

Cleo's Song

Eric, the girls, Tony - our world changed that day. I felt their suffering, a grief so deep inside, it made me numb, and I'll never be the same person again.

Someone told me that acceptance is the hardest stage of grief. I don't know if that's true for everyone, but it has been for me. Ivy's sudden passing has taken a toll on all of us. The incomprehensible thing out of all of this is I got a reprieve. Full remission. I received the stem cells from my best friend that same day. She was my perfect match in life as well as after. I got a second chance to do better... be better than I was. To love more, to serve more, to give more, and I did. There is an academic scholarship in her name at Bowman College. It's bittersweet because she never got to realize her dreams. The Ivy Brennan Women's Studies Building set among the magnolias near Higgins Hall, too.

Eric never would accept my money. I guess he was proud like that... or maybe he felt some sort of guilt. But he did allow me to bestow love and riches on the girls. All of the children, Tony, Nikki, and Erica, grew into amazing adults (never taking anything for granted) with families and careers that would make any mama proud.

I still keep in touch with Eric. We all get together on holidays with the kids. He's retired now... never remarried. Said he hadn't found anyone with Ivy's passion. I think he still misses her. I know I do. He lives in the same house where the loud rumbling of the Florence-Audubon freight train forges its way through the small town of Lawrenceville. If I had to categorize how our lives turned out, I would say the same thing that Ivy would have,

Toretha Wright

Blest be the tie that binds.
God blesses us all.
~ Cleo

A Note from the Author

I hope you enjoyed reading *Ivy's Passion* and *Cleo's Song*. Bits and pieces of this story were gleaned from my life and combed together to weave this tale of friendship so strong, time and distance could not crush it. I thank God, the source of my inspiration, for giving me the gifts to share this story with you. An honest effort went into its creation and execution. I find pleasure in knowing that my readers frequently ask when my next book is coming out. I try to oblige by writing whenever possible, and I hope to have new work coming to you soon.

Peace and blessings!

Toretha Wright

About the Author

Toretha Wright is a noted author of short stories and fiction novels. A South Carolina native, her literary works are set in small towns where her characters capture the charm of the South. The author has written and produced other literary works, such as poetry, prose, and theatrical plays that have been presented in a myriad of venues, winning awards and captivating audiences with her style of literary license.

Although Wright's works embrace different genres, her passion lies in southern and historical fiction.

Wright has received recognition in honor of Women's History Month and Black History Month for her accomplishments in literary arts. She was honored twice as a "Living Legend" for her "phenomenal writing." She received an International Book Award in Historical Fiction/Romance for her novel, *The Secrets of the Harvest*.

Her body of work includes poetry, novels, children's books, theater plays, and essays on the human condition. You can purchase her books at amazon.com and other online bookstores in traditional and ebook formats. For more information about the author, email torethawright@gmail.com.

Made in the USA
Monee, IL
14 October 2021